THE ULTIMATE TOP SECRET GUIDE TO TAKING OVER THE WORLD

BY KENN NESBITT

ILLUSTRATIONS BY ETHAN LONG

sourcebooks
jabberwocky

Published by Sourcebooks Jabberwocky, an imprint of Sourcebooks, Inc.
P.O. Box 4410, Naperville, Illinois 60567-4410
(630) 961-3900
Fax: (630) 961-2168
www.jabberwockykids.com

Library of Congress Cataloging-in-Publication data is on file with
the publisher.

Source of Production: Versa Press, East Peoria, Illinois, USA
Date of Production: February 2012
Run Number: 17143

Printed and bound in the United States of America.
VP 10 9 8 7 6 5 4 3 2

TO HERRON

CONTENTS

INTRODUCTION

Before you read this book, let's get one thing straight. You didn't hear any of this from me. I don't want people coming to me and complaining, "You never should have told that kid how to take over the world, because now we have to bow down before him or her and do his or her bidding!" (Which, you have to admit, is a pretty awkward thing to say.)

Nuh-uh. I've got enough headaches without having to listen to your whiny underlings griping about how diabolical you are, how you rule with an iron fist, and all that sort of sniveling.

So, Rule #1: You didn't hear any of this from me. Got it? As long as you remember Rule #1, you can read the book and we can still be friends, or at least not archenemies.

And whatever you do, *do NOT* run around telling all of your friends to buy this book. If you do that, your friends are going to want to become Evil Overlords too, and then they're going to tell their friends, who will then tell their friends, and I'll end up selling a million books and making lots of money and…Hang on a sec…

Forget everything I just said.

Rule #1: You heard this from me. Tell all your friends. Buy extra copies and give them as gifts to everyone you know. There. Now, as long as you remember Rule #1, you can read the book and we can still be friends. I mean *this* Rule #1, not the earlier Rule #1; you should have forgotten that one by now. Are we clear? Excellent.

Now that we've gotten Rule #1 out of the way, let me tell you a bit about this marvelous gem of a book you're holding. As you have probably already guessed from the title, this lovely little handbook is going to teach you everything you need to know to conquer the planet in ten easy steps. (Okay, so it might actually be thirteen or fourteen easy steps, but rounding it off to "ten easy steps" just sounds so much better, don't you think? I mean, honestly, who ever heard of doing anything in

me →  (VIII) "fourteen easy steps"? Not me. So if you see me fudging the numbers a little, just go with it.)

In fact, by the time you're done reading, and rereading, and, heck, let's just say *devouring* this wonderfully clever book (and telling all of your friends and buying lots of extra copies), you will have learned everything you need to know to have entire countries simultaneously groveling at your feet, chewing on their fingernails, and quaking in their baby booties. Seriously. You're going to learn all sorts of important stuff, including how to:

→ Become a genius overnight ✓

→ Think up your new Mad Scientist name ✓

→ Equip your underground lair ✓

→ Build evil robots ✓

→ Stop time for fun and profit ✓

→ Dress for conquest ✓

→ Clone mutant monsters ✓

→ Recruit minions ✓

→ Construct doomsday devices ✓

→ Defeat secret agents

→ Perfect your diabolical laugh → do not giggle

→ Choose your Mad Scientist theme song

→ Spend your first billion dollars

→ Do some other junk

Doesn't that sound insanely fantastic? Of course it does. That's why I wrote this book.

"But wait!" I hear you grousing. "If you know how to do all this amazing stuff, how come you don't rule the world yourself?" That's easy. I…uh…wait…uh…

Fine. I admit it. I'm too lazy. Happy now? I'd rather sleep in all morning and spend a couple of afternoons writing a book than lead battalions of nuclear destructo-bots in a quest for world domination. Which leaves the field wide open for you. All *you* have to do is read this book and carefully follow the instructions I've laid out, and in no time at all you will be laughing maniacally as the world cowers before you. Or something like that.

So if you're ready, let's begin.

> STEP 1 <

BECOMING
A GENIUS
OVERNIGHT

If you've decided to become an Evil Genius, you're probably not going to have too much trouble with the evil part. After all, you just have to decide to be rotten and despicable instead of good and kind, right?

No? How about this, then? You lose the one thing or person that means the most to you and feel that all of humanity is somehow responsible, ultimately going insane and vowing to take revenge on mankind by destroying all that is fluffy and cute in the world. Better? Excellent. See, I told you being evil wasn't hard.

The genius part, on the other hand, may seem a bit more challenging. You can't just decide to become ten times smarter and do it overnight, after all. Or can you?

In this chapter we'll look at some simple things you can do to increase your intelligence to genius levels with almost no effort.

If you're going to become a genius, we'd better define exactly what a genius is. If you look in any dictionary, you'll find lots and lots of pages, with many, many words on each page. It could take you several minutes just to find the word *genius*, and then several more minutes to read and understand the definition. Not a very smart use of time. On the other hand, if you just ask your mom what a genius is, she could probably tell you right away. If she can't, maybe you can get her to look it up and tell you what it says. That's still going to be quicker and easier than looking it up yourself.

So who's the genius? The person who wastes time looking things up in the dictionary or the person who gets other people to do the hard work for them? It doesn't take a genius to know the answer to that one.

While we're on the subject of moms, it's worth mentioning that until you create your first robotic slave or slobbering hunchback

NO DICTIONARIES! HA!

servant, your mom is the closest you're going to get to an actual lackey. That's right; moms cook for you, clean for you, shop for you, drive you around, and even buy you the occasional video game or candy bar. It's almost like having a maid, butler, chauffeur, and personal shopper all rolled into one.

Mom

But your mom's never going to raid the morgue for a fresh brain for your creature, and moms hate being told what to do. No, for that you're going to need a genuine minion. And that's another chapter. So let's get back to the subject at hand.

Need a minion

GRANDPA?

BECOMING A GENIUS OVERNIGHT

Oh, by the way, the actual definition of a genius depends a lot on whom you ask. Some people say you need an IQ of 180 to be a genius, while others claim you only need an IQ of 136. And still other people say that it doesn't matter what your IQ is; you just need to do something exceptionally creative (and be the very first person to do it) in art, science, etc. By that last defini-tion, I'm a genius for having writ-ten this book. See how easy it is?

Of course, it still took me a few after-noons to write this book, and that doesn't exactly qualify as "over-night." So we're going to need to speed things up a bit if you're going to be a genius by this time tomorrow.

▷ 1: EAT FISH

Ever heard the saying that "fish is brain food"?

How about, "You are what you eat"? What about, "Gimme your lunch money and I'll let you out of your locker"? Okay, so maybe you haven't heard that last one, but I have. And, trust me, if you ever did, you'd want to become a genius like me. So let's get back to those first two sayings.

"You are what you eat" doesn't mean that you are *literally* what you eat. If it did, you'd probably look like a big bowl of macaroni and cheese with a few chicken nuggets, a slice of pizza, and a handful of crayons. Nah. It just means that your body is *made out of* the stuff that goes in your mouth. Except for the part that comes out as poop, but I'd rather not talk about that. No, really. I mean it. I'd rather not talk about it, so stop asking, okay?

Which brings us to the other saying: "Fish is brain food." Believe it or not, something like half of your brain is made out of fish fat. Gross, right? Except that—and this is the cool part—the more fish you eat, the more brains you have.

Now, I know what you're thinking. Right now you're probably thinking something like, "I wonder if I could fit a whole pickle in my nose." Or maybe you're thinking, "I wonder if butterflies ever fart." But you shouldn't be thinking about stuff like that. You *should* be thinking about fish. And brains.

So here's what you have to do: Go ask your mom if you can have a tuna sandwich for dinner. When she says, "Yes," ask her if you can have fish sticks for dessert. When she says, "Are you feeling all right?" say, "Oh, look, Mom! What's that over there?" Then, while she's distracted, slip a can of sardines into your pants for later. Okay, well, not *in* your pants; use your pockets. Unless your pockets are too small. Or you don't have any pockets. In that case, just hold the can behind your back and whistle so you don't look like you're up to something.

But what if you don't like tuna, or fish sticks, or sardines? Hey, nobody ever said this was going to be easy. What's that? *I* said it was going to be easy? In this very chapter? Well, la de da. It *is* easy, as long as you like eating tuna, and fish sticks, and sardines. If you don't like tuna, fish sticks, and sardines, you'll have to try disguising the taste with lots of ketchup, or chocolate syrup, whipped cream, and M&M's. Or you could also try eating Goldfish crackers instead, but I don't think those work as well.

▷ 2: PLAY MORE VIDEO GAMES

"Turn that thing off! It's going to rot your brain!" Sound familiar? Funny thing is…it's not true. Video games actually make you smarter. No, really. I'm not just making that up. There are practically a bazillion very official research studies that show that kids who play the most video games are the smartest ones.

Okay, so there was really only one study that I know of, but still, that's better than *no* very official research studies, right? Oh, and I haven't actually seen that study, but I heard about it. Somewhere.

Anyway, these scientists studied a whole bunch of kids and discovered something that *you* probably could have told them if you weren't so busy trying to defeat the next boss level.

Namely, that video games:

1. Improve concentration

2. Improve problem-solving skills

3. Improve decision-making skills

4. Improve eye-hand coordination

5. Improve blah, blah, blah

6. Blah, blah, yadda, yadda, and so on, etc.

In other words, video games don't rot your brain. They *grow* your brain. They make you *smarter*. Which kind of makes you wonder…is someone you know trying to keep you from getting smarter? Hmmm…

And when you play video games, you are the one in control. You might just be controlling a bunch of falling blocks or a little yellow circle guy eating dots, or you might be controlling whole civilizations. No matter. You are the one in control. And that's something you're going to need to get used to if you're going to be in charge of the entire planet.

HA! CONTROL!!

Now, television, on the other hand...that *totally* rots your brain. It's nothing but commercials and goofy people doing dumb stuff. You'll never become a genius if you just sit around watching TV.

NOTE: BLOW UP TV!

Got it?

Stop watching TV. Play more video games. Soon you are going to rule the world.

▷ 3: MEMORIZE IMPORTANT-SOUNDING STUFF

Ruling the world doesn't actually require you to *be* a genius, as long as everyone *thinks* you're a genius. So how do you get everyone to think you're a genius? That's easy. All you have to do is memorize important-sounding stuff. And you don't even have to memorize things completely. You just have to remember more of the important-sounding stuff than other people.

Let's take pi, for example. Really, really dumb people think that pi is a kind of dessert with crust and filling. Normal people know that pi is actually a number, and that it is

approximately 3.14. Smart people memorize more digits of pi so they can show off how smart they are. Your typical smart person can rattle off pi to five digits, or 3.14159. So all you have to do to make people think you are a genius is to memorize pi to more digits than your typical smart person; seven digits ought to do the trick.

How do you memorize pi to seven digits? Easy. Just treat it like a phone number. Phone numbers are seven digits, and you remember your phone number, don't you? Just put a dash in the middle, like this: 141-5926. Repeat after me: 141-5926. 141-5926. 141-5926. Got it? Now you can say that pi is 3.1415926, and everyone will say you're a genius.

But that's just *ordinary* genius. If you want to show that you are a genius of staggering proportions—whatever that means—you'll need to memorize pi to ten digits. "How is that even possible?" I hear you gulp. Easy as falling off a bag of hundred-dollar bills. Just think of it as a seven-digit phone number in the 141 area code: 141-592-6535. Read and repeat: 592-6535. 592-6535. Now you can tell people that pi is 3.1415926535 and watch their jaws drop open. Then you can daydream about tossing peanuts into their open mouths, and try not to laugh; laughing would be rude.

What other impressive things can you memorize? How about learning the alphabet backward? It's not as hard as you think. You just need to have someone write it down backward for you. After all, why go to all that trouble yourself? In fact, since I slept in until noon today and I'm feeling rather generous, I'll do it for you:

Z Y X W V U T S R Q P O N M L K J I H G F E D C B A

Now you can sing the regular alphabet song, while reading the letters written above. It goes a little something like this:

ZEE WHY EX DOUBLE-YOU VEE YOU, TEE ESS ARE CUE PEE OH EN. EM ELL KAY JAY EYE AYCH GEE, EFF EE DEE CEE BEE AND AY.

I can sing my ZEE WHY EX'S. Now my brain's the size of Texas.

I'll give you one more for free. The atomic weight of uranium is 238, and the atomic weight of plutonium is 244. What does that mean? Who knows? But it sure sounds cool. And here's what I *do* know: Uranium and plutonium are used for making gigantic nuclear weapons. Sure, you could memorize the atomic weight of aluminum or helium if you wanted to, but then people would assume you were interested in soda cans or party balloons. Start talking about the atomic weight of plutonium, on the other hand, and, well, I think you get the idea.

LIST of NAMES
1. SPRINKLE DAISYFACE
NO
2. STACY McTINKLE
NO
3. EVIL OVERLORD JONES
MAYBE
4. DR. SINISTER McVONDERBRAIN
TOO LONG
5. KABOOM
TOO CIRCUS-Y
6. JONESY
DUMB

If you're going to rule the world, and do it right, you're going to need a new name. Don't get me wrong; I'm sure you've already got a perfectly solid name, and one you might even like, but let's face it, who ever heard of a Mad Scientist named Emma or Brandon? No, you need something truly diabolical-sounding; a name that will strike fear into the hearts of the foolish mortals who dare to even consider thwarting your plans for world domination. Stick with your boring old Michael or Hannah, and you might as well call yourself Captain Fluffy Bunny or Princess Sparkle Pony.

What you really want is something downright evil; a name that absolutely ripples with badness. Professor Death or Baron von Madness or something equally over-the-top. So here are a few simple rules to help you in your quest for the ultimate bad-guy name.

DEGREES AND TITLES

You don't have to be a real doctor to call yourself Doctor. After all, Dr. Seuss wasn't a real doctor. Of course, he wasn't a maniacal villain either, but that's sort of beside the point. Adding a title like "Doctor" or "Professor" to your name lends a certain gravitas. (*Gravitas*, by the way, means weightiness or seriousness, but it sounds a lot cooler.) It makes you sound like the genius you are, as if you've got a PhD in conquerology. And when combined with a wicked last name, the right title can make you sound like someone smaller countries shouldn't mess with.

Imagine being known as Doctor Destruction or Professor Sledgehammer. You see what I mean?

GIVING YOURSELF THE ROYAL TREATMENT

But wait! Before you run off and make yourself a doctor of devastation, let's look at some of your other options. Just as you can call yourself a doctor or professor without really being one, you can also give yourself a name that implies royalty. Here's how.

First, you need to recognize that not all royal titles are created equal. "King," "Queen," "Prince," "Princess," and even "Earl" and "Duke," are strictly for the good guys. King Evil just doesn't sound right, and even Princess Pain doesn't have a good ring to it. No, when it comes to being bad, the most worthy royal titles are "Count," "Countess," "Baron," and "Baroness."

These days no one can hear "Count" anything without thinking of Dracula. Of course, you can't be Count Dracula; that name's already been taken. But call yourself Count Heinous, and you instantly sound like the leader of a horde of rampaging demons.

Just as Dracula was a count, Frankenstein was a baron. That's right. In the classic 1931 horror film, Baron Victor

CALL HIM FOR MINION JOB

Frankenstein was the man who made the monster, and you, too, can use his title. You may also want to throw a "von" in the middle of your name, just for effect. Then dust off your thesaurus, find a suitable synonym for *badness*, and you can become the Baron von Damage.

Unlike "Doctor" and "Professor"—either of which can refer to a male or female—"Count" and "Baron" are only for boys. But that's okay. If you're a girl, "Countess" and "Baroness" can be equally unnerving. Countess Cruel and Baroness von Crusher sound like a couple of girls I would think twice about crossing.

Other titles worth considering are "Lord," "Lady," and even "Mister" or "Mistress."

"Lord" and "Lady" are especially good if you are an Evil Overlord, while "Mister" or "Mistress" are useful if you prefer a name that isn't all highfalutin.

And remember! Once you've given yourself a

royal title, your minions and other subjects will have to refer to you as Your Highness, at the very least. If you prefer being more creative, you can even think up more bombastic honorifics, such as Your Gloriousness or Your Most Magnificent Fantasticalness, or Your Very Evil Dastardliness.

GREAT NAME!

MILITARY TITLES

Oh, and let's not forget about military titles. Certain military titles are just as useful as academic and royal titles. Imagine being known as General Panic or Major Trouble.

But as with royal titles, some military titles are reserved for the good guys. Call yourself "Captain" anything, and you are instantly on the side of kindness and good.

And some military titles are really beneath you. You can't expect to rule the world as "Private" or "Corporal" or even "Lieutenant." You'll need to stick with the higher ranks if you expect people to do your bidding.

As a rule of thumb, "General" and "Major" are best. And they have the added bonus of double meanings.

General Disaster or Major Hurt aren't just names; they're descriptions!

"Colonel" and "Admiral" will work, too, as long as you have the right last name. Just don't tell people your name is Colonel Corn, or you'll never even be invited to join the worldwide bad-guy bowling league. Name yourself Admiral Bad, on the other hand, and folks might just wet themselves and run away crying like little babies. Okay, so little babies can't run, but they can wet them-selves and cry, and it would be really funny if they could run at the same time.

WHAT'S YOUR POWER?

If you have a bad-guy superpower, you can also name yourself after your power. But let's get one thing straight: if you're going to do this, you need to have a good power. Causing people to break out in irritating rashes is not the sort of thing people want from an evil world leader. No, it only works if you have the power to make stuff explode just by looking at it sideways. Or the power to create hurricanes by waving your pinky finger. Or the power to freeze time. Or turn people into gerbils.

Now, assuming that you've got a first-rate power, just add your title to the beginning, and you've now become Professor Hurricane, or Doctor Ice, or General Gerbil. Okay, maybe not General Gerbil, but you get the idea.

If you don't have any kind of bad-guy superpower, don't worry. All you have to do is put on a fake mustache and get a job as a janitor in a government research facility where you can have some sort of late-night accident with radioactivity or top-secret military technology. Next thing you know, you'll wake up in the hospital with a mutant ability worthy of an awe-inspiring new name.

THE TERRIBLE, THE HORRIBLE, AND THE BAD

Some bad guys like to add a little "the something" to the end of their names. Remember Attila the Hun? How about Ivan the Terrible? William the Conqueror? Robert the Bruce? Okay, well, as you can see, not all "the somethings" are created equal. You can't expect obedient followers if your name is Madison the Sweet, can you? Of course not.

Instead, start with a particularly wicked-sounding first name, such as Klaus or Sergei, and then tack on "the Terrible," "the Horrible," or "the Bad." Try these on for size: Turk the Terrible, or Magnus the Horrible, or Boris the Bad. See what I mean?

NOW IT'S YOUR TURN

Now that you know *how*, it's time to get out your pencil and a notepad and come up with your very own Evil Genius, world-ruling bad-guy name. In fact, because I am so thoughtful, I've even left you a few blank pages at the end of this book, so you don't have to go looking for a notebook or a blank sheet of paper.

So get your pencil, turn to the back of this book, and see how many scary-sounding Mad Scientist names you can think up. Just don't use the ones from this chapter. Those are mine. And they're copyrighted. And trademarked. And registered. Or something.

STEP 3

EQUIPPING YOUR
UNDERGROUND · LAIR

Every Evil Genius needs a quiet place to get away to plot the overthrow of humanity. And it doesn't get much quieter than underground. Call it your lab, your fortress, your bunker, your stronghold, your hideout, your sanctum, your lair. Call it whatever you want. Except Tiffany. Or Britney. That would be wrong in ways I can't even begin to describe.

But no matter what you call it, it's going to need a bunch of stuff if it's going to make a suitable base for planning your world conquest. Stuff like frozen pizzas. And cocoa with little marshmallows. And an extra-cushy chair. And, oh, yes, screaming robot ninja monkeys with flamethrowers and bazookas. Every good lair needs plenty of those.

Best of all, you don't even have to worry about what stuff you're going to need, because I'm going to tell you.

Think of this chapter as a handy checklist for the well-prepared dictator-to-be. An equipment guide for the tyrant in training. An indispensable reference for any  would-be master villain. Oh, heck. Let's just call it what it is: A shopping list for the criminally insane.

PUT YOUR LAIR UNDER THERE

Ha! Made you say, "Under where?" Okay, maybe not. Maybe you're too smart to fall for that one. I hope so. But if you're not, and you actually said, "Under where?" after I said "Under there," you probably should go back and read the chapter on "Becoming a Genius Overnight" one more time. It sounds like, in your case, it might take you two nights instead of just one.

Anyway, before you can equip your underground lair, you're going to need an actual underground lair to equip. And where's the best place in the world for an underground lair? Deep below the Rocky Mountains, with a mile or two of solid granite between you and your enemies. Down there nothing can get to you. Not even your aunt Beatrice's Christmas plum pudding that made you practically want to throw up at the dinner table last year. But you didn't. No, you just gulped and swallowed a whole bite. And you even smiled at Aunt Beatrice and tried not to cry and really, really tried not to throw up, because that would just be...What? That wasn't you? You don't even have an aunt Beatrice? Well, don't look at me. I don't have an aunt Beatrice either. I have an aunt Norma. And she makes Christmas plum pudding that doesn't make you want to throw up hardly at all.

So, yeah. Rocky Mountains. Dig straight down for a mile or two, carve out an acre of solid rock, install a high-speed elevator. Hold on. This is beginning to sound like actual work; not like an "easy step."

I've got a better idea. Instead of digging through miles of granite, why don't you build your fortress in the natural caverns below an extinct volcano on a remote Pacific island? Remote islands have lots of amazing features, such as white, sandy beaches and cold drinks with little umbrellas. And dead volcanoes are ideal for launching doomsday devices.

Still too much work? In that case, why don't you go and find yourself a nice used missile silo in Kansas instead? Those things have, like, twenty-foot-thick concrete walls to protect you and all your stuff. I heard they even sell them on eBay for only a few hundred thousand dollars.

Don't have a few hundred thousand dollars? Hmmm...I guess that only leaves one option. (Well, two if you count digging a hole in the backyard and covering it with plywood.) Yep. You're just going to have to commandeer your parents' basement. I know...

It's not nearly as cool as having an enormous, gadget-filled, secret chamber miles under the Rockies, complete with high-speed elevators, sentries at every entrance, and a jukebox that only plays your theme song. But hey, you've got to start somewhere, and—trust me on this one—I'm pretty sure most evil villains live in their parents' basements.

SECURING YOUR LAIR

Moving on, then. Now that we've decided you're going to move into the basement, and given that you don't have miles of granite or even yards of concrete to protect you, you're going to need to set up some basic security to keep the good guys from wandering in any time they feel like it.

The first thing you're going to need is a HEAVY STEEL DOOR. But since your basement doesn't have a HEAVY STEEL DOOR and only has a flimsy wooden door, you're going to at least need to make your flimsy wooden door *look* like a HEAVY STEEL DOOR. And how do you do that, exactly? With LOTS OF ALUMINUM FOIL AND SCOTCH TAPE.

BUT WHY, YOU ASK, AM I WRITING IN ALL CAPS? Really, it's just because the CAPS-LOCK KEY KEEPS GETTING STUCK and I'm MUCH TOO LAZY TO GET IT FIXED. so here. i did the next best thing. i hit it with a hammer and now it doesn't work at all. so the rest of this book is going to be written entirely in lowercase letters.

excuse me. the phone is ringing. i'll be right back.

thanks for waiting. that was my editor. she says i should get a new keyboard. i knew that.

Okay. New keyboard all plugged in.

We were talking about security. Wrap your basement door in aluminum foil and stick it on with Scotch tape. Perfect. Looks just like a heavy steel door, right? No? Well, just keep telling yourself that it does, and eventually you'll believe it. Maybe the good guys will believe it too.

Next, you're going to need security cameras so that if the good guys *do* try to break into your lair, they'll think they're being videotaped, and they'll worry about having spinach in their teeth and tripping over something and having the video show up on the Internet, and then they'll be all embarrassed and stuff when their moms see it and ask if they were at least wearing clean underwear. And all this worrying will make them so nervous that they will turn right around and go find some other villain to defeat.

But just in case they don't get all nervous and sweaty and run away whining like wiener dogs in a cactus patch, you're going to need one more important security measure: traps. What kind of traps, you ask? Why, BOOBY traps, of course. That's right. I said BOOBY traps. Repeat after me. BOOBY. Traps. Big BOOBY traps. Huge BOOBY traps. HEY! What are you laughing at? All I said was that you were going to need big huge BOOBY traps, and…Would you please knock that off?

Look, if you're going to keep snickering every time I say the word *BOOBY*…fine. I give up. Figure out how to make your own dang traps.

Instead, I'm going to tell you about the final security measure every underground lair needs: an escape route. Without it, you're a sitting duck. Your goose is cooked. You won't be able to fly the coop. You'll be singing your swan song. Your chickens will come home to roost. The early bird catches the worm. A bird in the hand is worth two in the bush. Why did the chicken cross the road? To escape, of course! The road was her escape route. What's yours?

The best escape route is a tunnel that leads into the forest, with the far end cleverly disguised as a bush. But since that's a long way from being an "easy step," you're just going to have to settle for the second-best escape route: the back door.

If your basement doesn't have a back door, you're going to need to figure out a way to disguise yourself as a piece of used stereo equipment so you can hide until you have a chance to sneak out the front door. Does your dad have some giant old speakers lying around from when he was the drummer for Iron Hamster, his high school heavy metal band, back before the iPod was

invented and everybody had long hair and smelled like goats? He does? Would he mind if you pulled the guts out of them to make a secret hiding spot? He would? Well, in that case, you're just going to have to get a big cardboard box, spray-paint it black, and hope the good guys are too dumb to tell the difference.

EVERYTHING ELSE YOU'LL NEED

Here is a complete list of everything else you will need to properly equip and furnish your fortress of inhumanity. You should plan to collect or build these things in your spare time, which I expect you will have lots of when your friends stop coming over after they find out you're living in your parents' basement.

→ **Consoles with lots of blinking lights.** Need I say more?

→ **Power generators.** Video games don't work after the FBI cuts the power, so plan on having emergency backup power if you can. If that's too much trouble, just be sure to hoard some extra AA batteries for your Gameboy/DS/PSP thingy.

→ **Interrogation chair.** This is just like a regular chair if a regular chair was bolted to the floor and had straps all over

 it to restrain your archenemy while you grilled him about the secret combination to the vault at Fort Knox.

→ **Bunk beds** for your minions and henchmen. Hey, you didn't think minions and henchmen deserved *real* beds, did you?

→ **Jail cells.** These are useful not only for locking up secret agents who try to thwart your plans, but also for holding any mutant monsters you create in your lab. If you have room for only *one* jail cell, well, the secret agents are just going to have to share that cell with your mutant monsters...if you catch my meaning.

→ **Survival gear.** In other words, big-screen TV, comfy couch, and lots of video games.

→ **Food.** I once met a guy who tried to live on nothing but Moon Pies. Really. He nearly

died after just three days from a lack of
sodium. Don't try it. Instead, be sure to
stock a good *variety* of foods that store well,
such as Fruit Roll-Ups, beef jerky, macaroni
and cheese, protein bars, and Gatorade. If
you have a freezer, and it's not already
full of lab specimens and alien body parts, I
recommend you stuff it with frozen pizzas.
Why? Because I like pizza, and
you should always have some
handy in case I come to visit.

→ **First-aid kit.** Hey, you never
know when you're going to get
a boo-boo.

→ **Klaxon.** What's a klaxon? It's a loud
electric horn. It's the kind of horn you hear
when the Starship *Enterprise* goes to red
alert level. The kind of horn you need, along
with a flashing red light, for when your
sister tries to enter your lair and you want to
annoy her into leaving. Klaxon. Get one.

→ **Bowling alley with disco ball.** Every world leader needs his or her own bowling alley. Even the White House has a bowling alley. The disco ball will give your bowling alley that extra little touch that says, "Yes, I'm a complete nut job, and I don't care who knows it."

→ **Loud countdown timer.** You'll want one that says official-sounding things like "Auto-destruct sequence initiated. T-minus-fifteen-seconds and counting. Help! We're all going to die! I want my mommy!"

→ **One very large rocket.** With steam coming out of the sides. Like in the early James Bond movies. Because, well, that's what villains do.

> STEP 4 <

EVIL ROBOTS 101

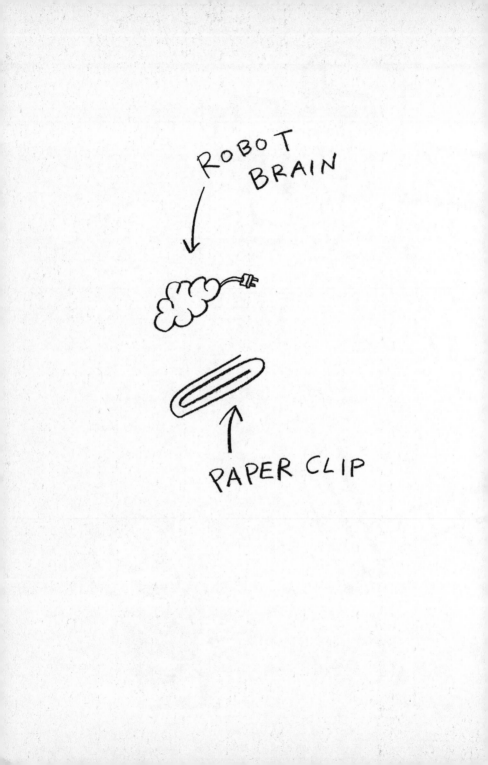

This chapter is a crash course on evil robots. That doesn't mean you're going to learn to crash evil robots, although I'll bet that would be fun too. No, it means I'm going to tell you everything I know about evil robots. And moderately bad robots. And slightly irritating robots. Yep. It's all right here. So sit back, tighten your restraining straps, and prepare yourself for a brief period of simulated education.

BIG BODY, TINY BRAIN

Every great evil robot needs two things: a GINORMOUS metal body and a teeny-tiny brain. The bigger the body, the more your robot is going to weigh, and the more it weighs, the more damage it can inflict on your arch nemeses. *Nemeses*, by the way, is the plural of *nemesis*.

Nemesis means enemy, and if you're reading this book, chances are that you are going to have lots of enemies, or nemeses. Your arch is the curve on the bottom of your foot, so an arch nemesis is an enemy that you want to step on. Or have your evil robot step on. And if you're going to have your evil robot step on your arch nemeses, it had better be a BIG evil robot.

ARCH

If your robot is big enough—say, a half ton or more, about the size of a slightly grumpy rhinoceros whose underwear is much too tight—it should be able to smash through brick walls.

A bit larger—perhaps the size of an irate T-Rex named Disco Floyd—and it can charge through vault doors, crush small automobiles, and even frighten the spooks at the Pickle Factory. Spooks, by the way, is an especially cool word for spies, and the Pickle Factory, I am told, is a nickname for the CIA—the Central Intelligence Agency. No, really. Don't ask me why; I have no idea. But it's such a ridiculous nickname that I just had to find a way to put it in the book.

SPOOK

Bigger still and your evil robot should be able to kick over tanks, swat fighter jets from the sky, knock down buildings, and generally stomp around like Godzilla in need of a diaper change.

BUT—and this is a really important BUT—in fact, this may be the most important BUT in the entire book. It's such an important BUT that I've written it in BIG letters. Like this: BUT. Hey! What's so funny? Are you laughing at my BIG BUT? Stop that! I told you, my BIG BUT is a very important BUT. I'm serious. Please stop laughing at my BIG BUT so I can tell you why it's such an important BUT.

BUT…okay fine. If you're not going to stop laughing at my BIG IMPORTANT BUT, I'm just going to have to make it an itty-bitty but. There. How do you like my itty-bitty but. What? Oh, sheesh!

BUTT ↓ Ɛ

AND—and this is a really important AND—you must not ever give your robot a brain any larger than that of your average garden slug. Have you ever seen the brain of a garden slug? Me neither. That's how I know that they are very, very small. Why, I hear you sniveling, must you not give your robot a brain any larger than the brain of your average garden slug? I was just getting to that, so stop your sniveling and pay attention. The reason is that evil robots *must* be simple-minded creatures with no room in their minuscule craniums for anything other than thoughts of crushing and destroying.

When you send your evil robot on a mission, it's not going to plunder graves for you or kidnap an heiress for the billion-dollar ransom. Those things require cleverness and quick thinking, so they are best left to your minions and henchmen. Evil robots are better suited to blowing stuff up with their laser eyeballs and overturning cars with robotic tentacles.

Now that we're clear—GINORMOUS metal body, teeny-tiny brain—let's move on.

SKETCHING YOUR ROBOT

Before you can build an evil robot, you're going to need to know exactly what it looks like. This means you're going to have to draw a picture of it. Because of my thoughtful and extremely lazy nature, I have left you several blank pages at the back of this book to sketch pictures of your evil robot.

In fact, I'm so thoughtful that I drew these pictures of robots for you so you can just sit and look at them instead of having to draw them yourself. I even drew some pictures of robot *parts*. That way you can tear a few pages out of the book, cut them up with scissors, and tape the pieces back together to try out different combinations of heads, bodies, limbs, and weapons. Or you can just cut them up and leave them lying on your bedroom floor for your mom to clean up.

BUILDING YOUR ROBOT

The first thing every good evil robot needs is a head. Robots without heads never look quite as evil as robots *with* heads. And eyes. Don't forget the eyes. You want your robot to be able to see where it's going and give the stink-eye to anyone it doesn't like (which is, of course, everyone but you).

When selecting a brain for your robot, I recommend using either the brain of a giant, slobbering, mutant lobster or your mom's toaster, whichever is more convenient. With so many would-be villains driving up the price of giant, slobbering, mutant lobster brains, I'm thinking the toaster might be easier.

Next you're going to need a body for your robot. Don't forget what I said earlier about how size counts when it comes to robot bodies. So look around your house for the biggest hunk of metal you can find. What is it? The kitchen garbage can? The lawn mower? The air conditioner? Dad's classic 1972 Buick Roadsmasher? I'm pretty sure it's okay to commandeer whatever you need as long as you plan to buy your parents a diamond-studded replacement after you reign supreme.

And, lastly, you're going to need some limbs. When you hear the word *limbs*, you probably think of trees. So do I. I think of lovely, majestic trees on a beautiful spring day, on a grassy hilltop, with their

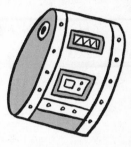

branches outstretched to the sky, being cut down by gigantic metal robots with chain saw hands and burning red eyes.

You see, *limbs* doesn't just mean tree limbs. It also means arms and legs. And in the case of evil robots, it means wheels, tank treads, chain saws, grenade launchers, laser cannons, razor-clawed metal tentacles, toilet plungers, fluffy bunnies, purple monkey cheese...okay, not really those last ones; I was just checking to see if you were paying attention.

Finally, now that you've picked out all the parts for your robot, you just need to stick them together. You *could* use a soldering iron, monkey wrench, blowtorch, sledgehammer, etc., but personally, I find it's easiest just to use duct tape. Everyone knows that duct tape is the universal solution to just about everything. In fact, I'm pretty sure that the only thing duct tape isn't good for is fixing ducts.

So get yourself a couple of rolls of duct tape and start building. When you're all finished, you should have something that looks like this.

Or this.

Or this.

Or this.

Okay, maybe not that last one. But you have to admit it's pretty evil.

TURNING YOUR ROBOT EVIL

Once you're finished building your robot, there's one last thing you have to do: turn it evil. I mean, if you just build it and then let it do whatever it wants, it might decide to become a landscape designer or a ballet dancer, and that just won't do. Robots are much cooler when they stomp around saying things like "Death. To. Humans." or "Crush. Kill. Destroy." than when they say things like "More. Petunias. Here." or "Slippers. Leotard. Tutu."

There are lots of different ways to turn robots evil, but here are a few suggestions for different ways you can try.

1. Give your Robot impossible instructions. Remember HAL 9000 from 2001: A Space Odyssey? No? Well, he was the space station's onboard computer, and take my word for it when I say he was homicidally insane. And why?

Because he was given conflicting instructions. He was constructed to be unable to lie or conceal anything, and then he was given orders to conceal an important discovery for reasons of "national security." He solved the problem by killing every human on board.

You can drive your robot over the edge in a similarly simple way. Tell it to make you a tuna sandwich without any tuna, or to clean the floor while wearing muddy boots, and watch as it is reduced to a quivering heap of paranoid schizophrenia (whatever that means).

The only trouble with the whole impossible instructions thing is that your robot might figure out that *you* are the cause of its problems and decide the best solution is to get rid of you.

2. Teach it about global warming. First explain to your robot how global temperatures are rising and the planet is at risk of dying. Then tell your robot that humans are the cause of

global warming. The solution is obvious. All. Humans. Must. Die. Except for you, of course.

3. Expose it to toxic waste and radioactivity. I've heard this works, though I'm not exactly sure where to get toxic waste and radioactive materials. Maybe you can take your robot on a tour of your local pesticide factory and nuclear power plant. Then, when no one is looking, push it over the railing into a vat of biohazardous sludge.

Once it drags itself out of the muck, hand it a pair of live electrical wires. The high-voltage shock will permanently fuse the toxic/radioactive goop into its circuits and, voila, instant evil.

4. Strap it to the couch and make it watch a *Barney and Friends* video over and over and over until its brains turn to mush from listening to Baby Bop sing "A-Camping We Will Go" for the thousandth time. In a matter

of weeks you'll have a lurching, lumbering, Frankenstein's monster of a robot.

Be warned, however, that if you use this technique, your robot may become too mentally unhinged to do anything but sit in the corner singing "B-I-N-G-O" and "Do Your Ears Hang Low?" If that happens, you'll just have to build a new robot and start over with a *Mister Rogers' Neighborhood* video instead.

5. Introduce it to a few terrorists, politicians, lawyers, used-car dealers, advertising salesmen, and roller disco instructors. Once it starts hanging out with these types, its sense of right and wrong will become so utterly distorted it won't stand a chance. Its brain will snap under the pressure, leaving it with such a permanently warped sense of reality that destroying everything in its path will seem like a completely logical thing to do.

EVIL ROBOT ARMY

The only thing better than an evil robot is an entire army of evil robots. So once you've finished building your first robot and turning it evil, it's time to build your second robot and turn it evil. In fact, if you do things right, you can get some of your evil robots to build even more evil robots while the other ones bring you cookies and scratch your back for you. The next thing you know, you'll have legions of evil robots waiting to do your bidding and take over the world for you.

Mwah ha ha ha ha ha ha! Snork!

STEP 5

STOPPING TIME FOR FUN AND PROFIT

YES!

ere it is. The one thing every would-be Evil Genius wants to know: how to stop time. And what to do once you've stopped it. I mean, seriously, what could possibly be more fun than running around doing a bunch of junk and stuff while everyone else is frozen in their tracks, completely unaware of your diabolical machinations.

Machinations, by the way, is a word that I used without knowing exactly what it means, just because I thought it sounded really cool. So I looked it up; I found out two things:

1. It's pronounced "mack-uh-NAY-shuns." That's good. I mean, it wouldn't sound nearly as impressive if it were pronounced "muh-SHEEN-uh-shuns," would it? And it would

totally stink if it were pronounced "eye-muhn-IHD-ee-uht" or "kihk-mee-RIHL-ee-hahrd."

2. Machinations are "crafty schemes, plots, or intrigues." Perfect. Now I don't have to delete it. As long as crafty means "Evil Geniusy" and not "macaroni and construction papery and gluey."

So, where was I? Oh, yes…stopping time. While everyone else is frozen. And you're running around doing a bunch of junk and stuff.

Welllllll…

THE GOOD NEWS

The truth is, I've got good news and I've got bad news. The good news is you *can* stop time. No, really. I mean it. You can. And you don't even need a time machine or a freeze ray or an expensive watch or anything like that.

The bad news I'll tell you later. After all, I don't want to ruin the rest of the chapter for you.

HOW TO STOP TIME

This is what you've been waiting for, reading through all of this ridiculous stuff to get to: instructions for stopping time.

1: Take those earbuds out of your ears. Turn off your video-game player. And put that chewing gum in the trash.

2: Do your homework.

3: Clean your room.

4: Go to the dentist.

5: Stand in the corner.

Right away you should notice something. As you stop listening to music, playing video games, chewing gum, or doing anything fun, time begins to slow down and everything takes much, much longer. You see, as everyone knows, "time flies when you're having fun." In other words, if you are enjoying yourself, time speeds up. What no one ever tells you, though, is that "time crawls when you're bored." That is, the less fun you are having, the slower time goes.

So all you have to do to stop time completely is stop having any fun whatsoever and be really, really, *really*, bored and miserable. Once you reach a state of infinite boredom and unhappiness, time stops completely and you are free to move about the world.

THE BAD NEWS

If you haven't already figured out the bad news, perhaps you should have your IQ checked for leaks. I mean, seriously, you can see the problem can't you?

The minute time stops and you start running around doing cool stuff, you'll be having fun again and time will stop being stopped…er…start.

So one second you're bored out of your skull and time has slowed to the point where the people in your family look like snails riding on turtles, and the next thing you know, you're laughing so hard at your family (after all, they look like snails riding on turtles) that time instantly speeds back up. And all because you just had to go and have some fun.

So the secret to proper time stoppage? Remain utterly bored for as long as possible. Do not under any circumstances allow yourself to have even the slightest bit of fun. Because the longer you can remain bored, the more fun you're going to have. Or something like that.

HOW TO REMAIN BORED AND MISERABLE

As with all things, when it comes to keeping yourself bored and miserable, there is, as they say, more than one way to skin a cat. I don't know why they say that, and in fact I don't even know who *they* are or why they would choose to say such a disgusting thing in the first place. But that *is* what they say. Or at least that's what they say that they say. I think.

So here are a few ways you can try to keep yourself from having any fun to ensure that time slows down and stays that way.

1. **Practice frowning.** In the same way that smiling can actually make you start to feel happy, frowning can make you feel sad. So go to the mirror and make the saddest face you can make. Now make the most bored face you can make. Now look depressed. Now roll your eyes like someone just said the stupidest thing you ever heard. Now roll your tongue. Now cross your eyes and stick out your tongue and... hold on...okay, you are obviously going to need

to be better at frowning than I am, so here are some other things you can try.

2. Ask your mom to serve you a big plate of overcooked Brussels sprouts for dinner. Trust me. Nothing slows down time like having to eat a big plate of overcooked Brussels sprouts. It might take only five minutes to eat them, but I guarantee it will feel like hours.

3. Read the dictionary. Start at the beginning and read the descriptions for every word, beginning with A. In no time at all, you'll be so bored that time will grind to a total halt.

4. Stare at a clock. Sort of. Okay, this one is a little different from the others, and doesn't require any boredom or inedible vegetables. Plus, this one actually stops time

for real, though maybe only for a few seconds.

need clock

First, you'll need a clock or a watch with a sweeping second hand. A digital clock won't work. You'll need a clock with a second

hand that moves smoothly rather than clicking from second to second.

If the clock in your classroom has a sweeping second hand, that's perfect. You'll be able to stop time in school.

Now stare at the second hand of the clock for five or ten seconds. Next, look just a little bit to the outside of the clock, fifteen or twenty seconds *ahead* of the second hand. If the second hand is pointing straight up, look to the right of the clock. If the second hand is pointing to the right, look below the clock. You can still see the second hand, even though you're not looking directly at it. And you will see that the second hand *stops moving for several seconds.*

Don't believe me? Try it yourself. Be prepared to be amazed. Once you get the hang of it, try counting in your head to see how long you can make time stop. With a little practice you can stretch it out longer and longer. Eventually...well, who knows?

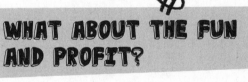

WHAT ABOUT THE FUN AND PROFIT?

I know, I know. The title of this chapter is "Stopping Time for Fun and Profit," and all I've done so far is talk about being bored and miserable. Well, hold on to your laser-guided chicken launcher, because here comes the fun part.

Once you've stopped time and can do anything you want, it's time to get busy. Now you can catch up on all those TV shows you have recorded, spend some quality time bouncing tennis balls off your brother's head, build a space station on the moon, and so on.

But first (which is the way I always jump into swimming pools), you really, really need to pull a few pranks. I mean, come on! Everyone is frozen in their tracks. You'll have time to put ketchup packets under every toilet seat in school.

Need some ideas for pranks? I'm only too happy to oblige. Feel free to try these around the house.

1. You know that sprayer hose next to the kitchen sink faucet? The one that shoots water out when you squeeze the handle?  No? Here. Let me draw you a picture.

For this prank, all you're going to need is one simple rubber band. It's best if you can find one that's not red. Red ones are easier to spot.

With the water turned OFF, take your rubber band and stretch it around the faucet handle several times so that it holds the handle in. Then set the faucet hose back and turn it so that it's pointing straight out. Like this:

The next time someone turns on the kitchen sink, kablooie! They get sprayed. And hopefully "they" is your sister.

2. Want to drive your parents crazy? This prank is so simple and doesn't even require a rubber band. Go to your parents' computer and unplug the mouse from the back. That's it. Leave the mouse right where it belongs and don't do anything else.

The next time one of them sits down to use the computer, they'll go nuts trying to figure out why the mouse isn't working. They'll probably reboot the computer. When that doesn't work, they might even call tech support.

When they finally figure it out and plug the mouse back in, they'll be puzzled, but they probably won't suspect it was you. When they are away from the computer, unplug it again. This fun little prank can go on for days.

3. Reset all the clocks in the house. This prank is easy to do and can cause lots of chaos, especially if you do it right.

Most importantly, you need to reset every clock in the house to the same time. If you set them to different times, or random times, everyone will figure it out pretty quickly. But if you set every clock in the house ahead by, say, thirty-seven minutes, and all to the same time, everyone will be early for work or school and no one will know why.

If your parents wear wristwatches, it's important to reset those as well, which is why it's useful to be able to stop time before embarking on this little bit of mischief.

4. Switch the foods in the kitchen. For example, fill the salt shaker with sugar and the sugar bowl with salt. The next time anyone puts a spoon of sugar on their cereal or sprinkles salt on their eggs...well, you get the idea. You can put hot sauce in the ketchup bottle, vinegar in bottles of drinking water, horseradish in the mayonnaise, and so on. Basically, if two foods look alike, swap them and then go about your day.

If you want to be really dastardly, try this with a package of OREO cookies: for each cookie

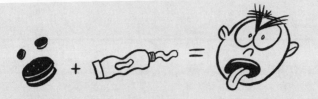

in the package, twist the cookie open, eat the frosting out of the middle, replace the frosting with white toothpaste, and put the cookie back. The next person who eats an Oreo is in for a big surprise. Be warned, though; some people don't think this is as funny as I do.

AND THE PROFIT?

Remember what I said in the last chapter about the secret combination to the vault at Fort Knox? Well, Fort Knox is where the government keeps all of their gold. Once you have the combination and you can stop time, you can simply tippy-toe into Fort Knox and waltz back out with a billion dollars' worth of shiny gold bars.

Now you'll have enough money to buy that new XGameStation you've been drooling over. You could even get one with no drool on it. Oh, and you could buy your first country. Isn't villainy fun?

> STEP 6 <

DRESSING FOR
CONQUEST

STOPPPPPP!! This is *exactly* what no self-respecting villain *ever* wants to hear. Just as you're going to need a new name if you want to be taken seriously, you're also going to need a new set of duds. Jeans and a T-shirt might work for you at school, but they are guaranteed to get you defenestrated from the International League of Super Criminals faster than you can say, "What the heck does 'defenestrated' mean?"

Defenestrated, by the way, is one of the best big words you'll ever learn, so you might as well learn it from me. Peppering your sentences with phrases like "Defenestrate that nemesis, minion" will ensure that everyone knows what a genius you are. And defenestrating your enemies is one of the most satisfying ways of eliminating them.

So what does "defenestrated" mean? Why, it means to be thrown out of a window. You can defenestrate enemies, furniture, schoolbooks, Barney the singing dinosaur, or anything else you find annoying and want to be rid of. Just give it the old heave-ho and out the window it goes.

As I was saying, if you don't want to be thrown out of a window at the International League of Super Criminals, you're going to need to come up with a better look than whatever it is you're wearing right now. That means you're going to need a new outfit, new foot-wear, new headgear, a new hairstyle, and maybe even a mask or some extremely cool glasses. Stick with the T-shirt and jeans, and you'll never be more than an

ordinary, run-of-the-mill hoodlum. Choose the right look, on the other hand, and soon the entire world will be singing your theme song.

WHAT KIND OF A VILLAIN ARE YOU ANYWAY?

But before you can decide which fashions are going to make you look the most dastardly, you are going to have to decide exactly what kind of a villain you are. After all, Mad Scientists don't usually wear purple spandex jumpsuits, super-villains tend not to prefer black armor, and evil overlords aren't often attired in white lab coats. To help you decide what *you* should wear, here are a few of the more well-known villain types and the outfits they tend to choose.

BLACK HAT

This guy is your basic, everyday, clichéd, cartoony villain. The Black Hat wears black clothes, a black cape, and a black top hat, and always has a long, black handlebar mustache suitable for twirling. To distract the hero while he escapes, he ties helpless maidens to railroad tracks and then wrings his hands and cackles with glee as the onrushing train approaches.

Although no other villain types look quite as dastardly as the Black Hat, it's worth noting here that THIS GUY IS AN IDIOT! Sorry. I just had to get that out of my system. You should never aspire to be like him. He commits petty crimes like robbing stagecoaches and kidnapping helpless maidens to tie to railroad tracks. And every time he is defeated by the guy in the white hat, he says ridiculous things like "Curses! Foiled again!"

But if in your heart of hearts you know you were just meant to be nothing greater than a stock silent-movie villain, you'll need the following: One black suit with a black shirt and pointy black boots. One black cape, but make sure it's a waist-length cape and not a long one like superheroes wear. One black top hat. One long, black mustache and a can of mustache wax so you can make it all curly on the ends. One black satchel for carrying safe-cracking tools, ropes, and a picnic lunch in case the stagecoach is all out of sandwiches.

EVIL RULER

Now, this is more like it. If you're going to take over the world, it helps to be a megalomaniac, which means being obsessed with wealth, power, genius, fame, small furry creatures, and so on. If you can imagine yourself standing atop a pyramid wearing sun-god robes while throngs of worshippers bring you stacks of gold and lots of Sour Patch candies, you'll probably make a fine Evil Ruler.

evil ruler

Remember Jafar from the Disney film *Aladdin?* Evil Ruler. How about Yzma from *The Emperor's New Groove?* Definitely Evil Ruler. Plankton from *SpongeBob SquarePants?* Evil Ruler for sure. Mr. Noodle's brother, Mr. Noodle from *Sesame Street?* Okay, maybe not Mr. Noodle, but wouldn't it be cool if Mr. Noodle decided to become an Evil Ruler? I think so too.

Being an Evil Ruler also gives you lots of flexibility in what you wear. Most Evil Rulers prefer to dress like kings, queens, and high priests of ancient times. That means fancy robes and headgear, billowy pants, magical staffs, shiny bling…you get the idea. Use your imagination, go a little wild, and dress to impress.

MAD SCIENTIST

In case you were wondering, this is what I look like normally.

Mad Scientists often start off as normal scientists, but become obsessed with their experiments to the point where they go crazy. Whether they are tinkering with time or gravity, or trying to reanimate the dead, they feel completely misunderstood and unappreciated enough that when they snap they often want revenge on all of mankind. I'm getting my revenge on the world by writing this book.

If you feel you are also the Mad Scientist type, here's what you're going to need to complete your outfit.

Love the gloves.

→ Long, white lab coat. The rest is optional, but every Mad Scientist needs one of these. Without it, you're just mad, not a scientist.

→ The right hairdo. Most Mad Scientists are either bald or have crazy white hair. You could get a bald cap from a costume shop, but it's crazier to just shave your head. If you prefer the crazy white hair look, you're going to need a Mad Scientist wig, assuming you don't already have crazy white hair.

→ Black lab gloves. These should be big, black safety gloves, made to resist chemical spills, toxic waste, and the tears of your pitiful victims.

→ Doctor's head mirror or welding goggles. With a doctor's mirror on your forehead, you'll look like you are ready to perform surgery at the drop of a hat. With a pair of heavy-duty welding goggles strapped to your head, you'll look like you are always ready to perform  reckless experiments with lightning and green bubbling goo. No need to actually put these over your eyes. Really. They're just for show. The forehead is fine.

→ A very technical-looking weapon. You'll probably want some sort of handheld laser cannon, ice ray, time disrupter, etc. I recommend you make your own so that your enemies don't think you're just carrying a Nerf gun or a Super Soaker.

→ Other junk to make you look a little nutty. Use your imagination here. Not only do you want an ID badge and lots of pens and pencils in your

lab coat pocket, but feel
free to include food
stains, burn marks,
cheese sandwiches, rubber
frogs... You get the idea.

EVIL GENIUS

You're probably thinking that an Evil Genius and a Mad Scientist are the same thing, but that's not always true. An Evil Genius is simply a super-intelligent person who has decided to use his or her gift for evil instead of good. Remember Lex Luthor from the *Superman* comics? Dr. Evil from *Austin Powers*? Stewie from *Family Guy*? All Evil Geniuses. None are Mad Scientists.

So what do Evil Geniuses wear? Well, let's see. Lex Luthor wears a suit. Dr. Evil

wears a suit. Stewie wears red overalls with a yellow shirt. So what should *you* wear? Anything you want. Remember, you're the smartest person on the planet. Whatever you decide to wear is the right thing. But if you want my opinion, go with the (suit.)

Buy a suit.
Ask Dad
for $$$.

SUPER-VILLAIN

Not satisfied being your ordinary, run-of-the-mill villain? Aspire to something greater or maybe something flashier than just being unbelievably smart (and evil)? Perhaps you should consider becoming a Super-Villain.

Super-Villains are just like regular villains except they get to wear much niftier costumes. Some Super-Villains have superpowers, just like their superhero nemeses, so, just like superheroes, they also need to wear spandex outfits to show off their muscles, make it easier to fly through the air, shoot fireballs from their fingertips, or do whatever it is they do. What's spandex, I hear you ask? Why, it's that stretchy stuff that superhero costumes are made out of. Just make sure you don't wear it unless you've got the muscles underneath, or some awfully convincing padding.

Other Super-Villains lack any sort of actual superpower but make up for it by having an especially clever gimmick or lots of awesome gadgetry. These sorts

of Super-Villains usually wear flashy outfits—such as purple velvet suits—have colorful hairstyles, and smile just as demonically as the villains with superpowers. They just don't get to wear spandex; they don't spend enough time in the gym.

When choosing a color for your Super-Villain outfit, just remember that blue and yellow are mostly reserved for the good guys. You want to stick with black or red, the colors of evil. If you are feeling more flamboyant, green or purple, or even green *and* purple, are also good choices.

EVIL OVERLORD

Man! Who knew there were so many different types of villains? And their names are so similar that it's hard to keep them straight. I mean *Evil Overlord* sounds just a little too much like *Evil Ruler* or *Evil Genius*. But there *is* a difference. Really.

The Evil Overlord is also known as a "dark lord," and their power usually comes from magic. Their minions are usually orcs and goblins and other nasty magical beasts. Because of this, if you are an Evil Overlord wannabe, you're going to want to wear armor. Black armor. And a cape. I also recommend a face-concealing helmet with wicked-looking horns on it. And a sword. A big sword. And a banana. A big, scary-looking banana. Okay, not really. I wasn't serious about the banana. But the rest of it's good.

TIN-POT DICTATOR

First you take charge of the army, and then you have the army kick out the president for you and, voilà, you're a Tin-Pot Dictator. It helps if you believe that you are much more important, famous,  and powerful than you really are. Tin-Pot Dictators, in case you're wondering, get their name from the funny little general's hats they wear that look like tin pots on their heads.

If you are going to rule the world as a Tin-Pot Dictator, you're going to need the appropriate outfit—in this case, a general's uniform with lots of medals, ribbons, badges, gold fringe, and other junk like that. The more stuff you have on your uniform, the more you'll look the part of a Tin-Pot Dictator. And the more you look the part, the better chance you'll have of ruling the world instead of sitting on the curb using your tin-pot hat to beg for change.

STEP 7

OF MONSTERS
AND MINIONS

island

man

As the poet John Donne once famously said, "No man is an island." Well, duh! Of course no man is an island! I mean, who ever heard of a human island. I heard of a guy once who thought he was a canary. And there was a book about a guy who thought his wife was a hat. But an island? And who is this John Donne guy anyway? As Bugs Bunny once famously said, "What an embezzle! What an ultra-maroon!" Whatever that means.

Well, you may not be able to *be* an island, but you could certainly *own* one. Or a whole bunch of islands. Islands are the perfect place to hatch your plot to take over the planet. Not only are islands the only suitable locations for building island fortresses, but they are also excellent places to clone armies of mutant monsters.

See, you don't want just *one* mutant monster. Try to take over the world with a single mutant monster, and you'll be the laughingstock of the villain community. After your monster is handily dispatched by the forces of good, you'll wind up on some dusty, low-traffic street corner holding a sign that reads, "WILL TAKE OVER THE WORLD FOR FOOD."

So you're going to need an entire army of mutant monsters. This takes two steps:

1. Create a mutant monster.

2. Clone it over and over again.

3. Instruct your monster army to eat your enemies.

4. Do not let your monsters eat you.

5. Okay, I realize this is more than two steps.

6. But I'm really enjoying writing this way.

7. Okay, I'll stop now.

HOW TO MAKE A MUTANT MONSTER

Great title. It really is the ULTIMATE!

Remember, you don't just want a regular monster, you want a *mutant* monster. Luckily, there are several tried-and-true ways of creating a mutant, including:

→ Large doses of Radiation

→ Weird chemicals

→ Mixing DNA from different creatures

→ Any combination of the above

Combining radiation, chemicals, and DNA is the best way to get the results you want. For example, try blasting a tarantula with gamma radiation while bathing it in green slime. Or practice teleporting the dog along with a housefly so that their DNA mixes together.

Or feed your dad's cooking to the cat. All of these are
pretty much guaranteed to create freakishly grotesque
and bizarre monsters never before seen on earth.

Radiation

It also helps if a UFO accidentally crashes
in your backyard. UFOs are loaded with radiation, weird chemicals, and, best of all, *alien*
DNA. Just remember, when handling alien DNA
and weird chemicals, you should always wear rubber
gloves, safety goggles, a surgical mask, lab coat, knee
pads, party hat, floppy shoes, red rubber nose…Wait.
Sorry. Those last ones are only required when handling
clown DNA, which, by the way, is equally nasty.

Another great way to create a mutant monster is to
start from scratch. First you'll need a drop of blood or
a skin cell or a strand of hair from a regular monster

like, say, your sister. Put this in a test tube with a mutation agent such as cobra venom, moldy rotten cheese, sweaty gym socks, your math homework, a Teletubbies video, or something equally horrible and dangerous. Then you mash them together really well, add a bit of water and sugar, and leave it in a warm, moist place like the bathroom or your laundry hamper. Pretty soon it will start to fester and grow into something with too many eyes, creepy tentacles, and a smell worse than your brother's breath after a garlic and liverwurst sandwich. In other words, perfect.

CLONING YOUR MUTANT MONSTER

Once you've got your first mutant monster, you're going to need to make more of them. Lots more. Thousands more. Enough to threaten the world and be taken seriously as the power-hungry, criminally insane genius you are.

And what's the easiest way to turn one evil freak of nature into thousands? Why, cloning of course. Cloning is copying, but you can't exactly stuff your mutant monster into the Xerox machine at your local copy shop and spit out clones at a nickel apiece. I'm pretty sure it's more complicated than that.

So how do you clone a mutant monster, exactly? I have no clue. So I did the first thing I could think of. I asked my mom. She didn't know either. So I looked it up on the Internet and read all about it. And you know what I found out? Cloning is easy.

It turns out, to clone an animal, all you have to do is take a bit of its DNA and use it to fertilize an unfertilized egg. Then the egg will grow into an exact copy of the animal.

So here's what you do:

1. Get a drop of blood or a skin cell or a strand of hair from your mutant monster.

2. Get an egg from the refrigerator and make sure you don't accidentally get any fertilizer on it (so it remains "unfertilized").

3. Under a microscope, remove the nucleus (or middle) of a single cell of the blood, skin, or hair.

4. Sprinkle the cell nucleus (which contains the DNA) over the egg to fertilize it, kind of like fertilizing your lawn.

5. Do this with one thousand more eggs.

6. Go about your business making plans for world domination.

In no time at all, you'll have lots of little baby mutant monsters calling you "Mama" or "Dada" and wanting to chew your toes off.

AND DON'T FORGET YOUR MINIONS

I looked up *minion* in the dictionary just to make sure it didn't mean something like "miniature onion," and, sure enough, the dictionary said, "A servile follower of a person in power." Who's the person in power? You are. Who's the servile follower? Your minion. Who's the leader of the club that's made for you and me? M-I-C-K-E-Y M-O-U-S-E!

Anyway, as I figure it, the more servile followers you have, the more that makes you the person in power. In other words:

More Minions = More Power

YES!!!

So you want to have lots of loyal minions.

Booty

Minions are useful for lots of stuff, but mostly for plundering and bringing you the booty. You want lots of minions so they can bring you lots of booty. BIG BOOTY. SHINY BOOTY. So you can laugh and dance on your BIG, SHINY BOOTY. And roll around on the bed with your booty. And throw your booty in the air. And shake your booty like you just don't care.

And...Hey! Stop that! Are you laughing at the BIG, SHINY BOOTY? You are? Hmmm...

On second thought, don't stop. It's okay to laugh at the BIG, SHINY BOOTY, as long as it's a maniacal laugh, a laugh that will send chills down the spines of your enemies, a laugh worthy of your stature as the Dictator of the World. But that's a subject for another chapter. In the meantime, keep laughing. Booty booty.

Now, where was I? Oh, yes. Minions. First, it is important to recognize that there are different types of minions, and you are going to want as many of each kind as you can get to serve you.

▷ FLUNKIES AND LACKEYS

Flunkies and lackeys are servants who do your bidding, especially when it doesn't require brains or muscles. They are great for delivering messages, bringing you milkshakes and pillows, and calling you "Master."

You'll want lots of these so that they can run around doing all the stuff that you're too lazy to do yourself.

▷ GOONS, THUGS, AND HENCHMEN

Goons and thugs are also like flunkies and lackeys, but with muscles. Henchmen are like flunkies and lackeys, but with weapons. All three of these types of minions are useful for delivering messages like, "Da boss says he wants his money by Toosday, or he'll be very unhappy. And when da boss is unhappy, I'm unhappy. And you really don't want to see me unhappy."

Because they're good at scaring people, they're also good at petty crime, like snatching candy from babies and stealing nuclear warheads from the government.

As with flunkies and lackeys, you can never have too many goons, thugs, and henchmen.

▷ GRUNTS

Grunts are sort of like goons and thugs, but they have even bigger muscles and they're much too dumb to deliver messages. Grunts are better suited for digging tunnels and carrying heavy crates. Especially crates filled with BIG, SHINY BOOTY.

▷ ICE CREAM VENDORS

Okay, so ice cream vendors aren't really a kind of minion, but if you can get one to do your bidding, you can have ice cream anytime you want. So I recommend you try. By the way, if you figure out how to get an ice cream vendor to do your bidding, would you please let me know so I can have one too? It's such a pain having to put my slippers on and shuffle down to Dairy Queen all the time.

WHAT ALL MINIONS HAVE IN COMMON

Now, the one thing you will notice that all types of minions have in common is that they are dumb. Really,

really dumb. This is good. You don't want your minions thinking. You want minions who will believe anything you tell them and follow orders without questions.

Your ideal minion is not the sharpest knife in the drawer. Not the brightest bulb on the Christmas tree. A few bricks short of a load. As sharp as a bowling ball. A few fries short of a Happy Meal. Fell out of the stupid tree and hit every branch on the way down. A few clowns short of a circus. Doesn't have both oars in the water. One taco short of a combination plate. The elevator doesn't go all the way to the top floor. The lights are on but nobody's home. As dumb as a stump. As dumb as a sack of hammers. So dumb he couldn't pour water out of a boot with instructions on the heel. Any dumber and you'd have to water him. And, trust me, that's dumb.

But why, I hear you muttering, should you only want minions who are so dumb it takes them an hour to make Minute Rice? What's so great about a minion who stares at the orange juice because it says "concentrate"? Why get a minion who is so dumb he thinks you can't listen to AM radio in the afternoon? Because when minions are this dumb, you can tell them, "I'll pay you tomorrow" every day and they'll never catch on.

So where do you find minions this dumb? Easy. Put an ad in the paper offering to pay a million dollars a day for very little work. Anyone dumb enough to believe this is dumb enough to be your minion.

YOUR RIGHT-HAND MAN

There is *one* type of minion you will need who is not as dumb the rest, and that's your right-hand man, also known as your "trusted lieu-tenant" or your "number one." Your right-hand  man is the servant who tells the rest of your flunkies, lackeys, goons, thugs, henchmen, grunts, ice cream vendors, and even your mutant monsters what to do while you play video games and think of clever and inventive ways to destroy the world.

Of course, you're not actually *going* to destroy the world. You're just going to think of clever and inventive ways that you *could* destroy the world so that you can *threaten* to unleash your deathtastic, kill-o-rific doomsday device if you aren't paid a kajillion dollars in gold bricks. But that's a subject for another chapter.

Ideally, your right-hand man should be smart (but not as smart as you) and greedy. The lure of lots of big, shiny gold bricks—someday in the future—should be enough to keep him loyal to you, especially if you share your ice cream vendor with him.

LEGIONS OF TERROR OR CUPCAKE CAMPERS?

Altogether, your right-hand man, your minions, your army of mutant monsters, and your evil robots form what is commonly referred to as your "Legions of Terror." Personally, though, I don't think you should call them Legions of Terror. I think you should call them Cupcake Campers or Rainbow Fairy Brotherhood so that no one will suspect their imminent destruction.

After all, if you tell a country you are sending your Legions of Terror for a visit, you might meet with some resistance. But if you tell them you are sending your Sparklytown Girls' Choir for a "song festival," they'll greet you with open, and unsuspecting, arms. Then you can walk in, take over the throne, rename the country in honor of yourself, and begin building your new, worldwide empire.

← me

MY WORLDWIDE EMPIRE!

STEP 8

YOUR FIRST DOOMSDAY DEVICE

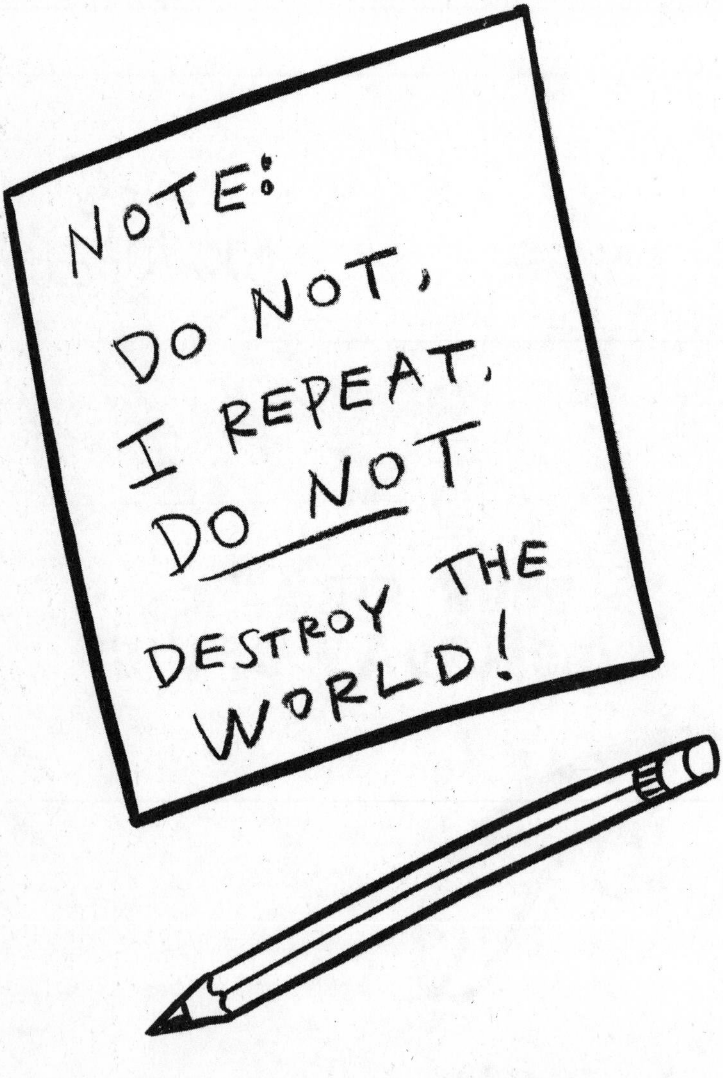
NOTE:
DO NOT,
I REPEAT,
DO NOT
DESTROY THE
WORLD!

efore I teach you how to destroy the world, let me make this very clear. Do NOT destroy the world. You are absolutely under no circumstances to actually destroy the world. Is that clear? After all, I live here. If you destroy the world, where I am going to lie out by the pool drinking icy drinks with little umbrellas in them? Exactly. Nowhere. Which will make me very, very grumpy.

And if you destroy the world, how are you going to be able to rule it? Right. You won't. So don't do it. Got it?

Now, you might rightfully ask why I would tell you how to destroy the world if you can't actually do it. Fair enough. You see, the easiest way to *take over* the world is to *threaten* to destroy the world. And if you're going to threaten to destroy the world, you need to know how to actually do it. Otherwise people will just laugh at you, and you won't even be able to rule the hall closet or the bathroom.

So here we go…

HOW TO DESTROY THE WORLD

When I say "destroy the world," I don't actually mean "destroy the world." "Destroy the world" is just a shorthand way of saying…"Help! There's a hamster in my undies!"

Sorry about that. My sister stuck a hamster in my undies and then ran away laughing. I didn't mean that "destroy the world" was really another way of saying, "Help! There's a hamster in my undies!"

What I *meant* to say was that "destroy the world," is a shorthand way of saying, "make the world uninhabitable for humans." In other words, you don't necessarily have to threaten to blow the world to pieces, or to smithereens, or to kingdom come, or into next Tuesday, or anything like that; you just have to threaten to destroy all human life on earth.

Fortunately, there are lots and lots of ways to make the world uninhabitable for humans. Heck, you're probably doing some of them right now. For example, did you leave your bedroom light on? If so, you're contributing to global warming, which eventually may cause glaciers to thaw, sea levels to rise, forests to become deserts, Popsicles to melt, butter to become un-spreadably soft, and other such disasters.

The problem is, you can't just threaten to leave your bedroom light on. It's only a problem when *everybody* leaves their bedroom light on, and, even then, it might take decades for anything bad to happen. So no one will take you seriously. They might point and snicker, or roll their eyes and call you names, but they won't take you seriously.

On the other hand, if you build a giant gravity machine capable of pulling the moon closer to the earth, the increased gravitational pull of the moon will cause tidal waves, tsunamis, typhoons, earthquakes, and people will run around waving their hands in the air and crying like little babies with diaper rash. And they'll take you seriously. As seriously as little babies take diaper rash.

In other words, even though your bedroom light may someday make the world uninhabitable by humans, it is *not* a genuine doomsday device. A giant gravity machine, on the other hand, *is* a genuine doomsday device, and not a bad one at that, if I do say so myself.

So here are several ideas for doomsday devices you can build and other ways that you can…"Help! There's a hamster in my undies!"

Excuse me while I go give my brother an atomic wedgie.

DOOMSDAY DEVICES YOU CAN BUILD AND OTHER WAYS THAT YOU CAN "DESTROY THE WORLD"

When building doomsday devices, it's best to think big. Really, really big. Like pulling-the-moon-closer-to-the-earth big. And flashy. Like disco-ball-and-purple-sequined-jumpsuit flashy. Big-and-flashy ideas are good attention-getters. Small-and-ordinary ideas, on the other hand, are *not* good attention-getters. To take over the world, you first need to get everyone's attention. All of the following ideas are of the big-and-flashy sort, just perfect for someone like you.

▷ BLOW UP THE MOON ≥KABOOM!≥

This one's almost too easy. You may have heard that NASA (which I believe stands for Neil Armstrong's Space Agency) is sending rocket ships to the moon, loaded with explosives. They want to detonate bombs on the moon so that they can study the dust that's kicked up to see if there's any water under the surface. I'm not sure why they can't just go to the drinking fountain down the hall, but whatever.

All you have to do is sneak into NASA (which I believe stands for National Association of Space Alligators) headquarters and put a bigger bomb on the rocket that they're sending to the moon. That way NASA's rocket will blow up the moon and giant chunks of it will rain down on earth, destroying Las Vegas and Paris and

Mount Rushmore and Disneyland and your house and my house and so on and so on.

Just please make sure that you have a remote control handy so that you can blow up the rocket before it gets to the moon. That way the government will give you eleventy bajillion dollars and elect you Emperor of the Planet to stop you from blowing up the moon.

▷ GIANT SPACE LASER

This one's a little trickier, but probably more fun. As long as you're sneaking into NASA (which I believe stands for Norman Ate Seven Aardvarks), you can put a giant laser on that rocket headed for the moon. I recommend putting it on one of those moon rover buggy things and reprogramming it so you can remote-control it from your Nintendo.

Once your giant laser lands on the moon, you can point it at the earth and blow up important stuff like the

Hoover Dam, or the Great Wall of China, or the Panama Canal, or the factory in New Jersey where they make all the M&M's. Once the M&M's factory is destroyed from space, they'll know you're serious and give you anything you want.

▷ CREATE A BLACK HOLE

Check this out. I heard that they have this lab in Switzerland where they smash subatomic particles into one another at nearly the speed of light and they expect to make teeny-tiny, little black holes.

Now, a black hole, as everybody knows, is kind of like a doughnut hole, only black. And not nearly as tasty. Black holes are black because their gravity is so strong that they suck in everything around them, including sugar, and cinnamon, and chocolate frosting, and rainbow sprinkles, and your next-door neighbor's poodle, and telephone poles, and Duluth, Minnesota, and even light itself. But the black holes they're going to make in Switzerland—because they are made by

● ← Black Hole

smashing extremely small particles together—are only going to be big enough to suck in tiny things like specks of dust and the brains of garden slugs.

You can fix this. All you have to do is sneak in and set the machine up to smash a couple of big things together—say, a cow and a minivan—at nearly the speed of light, and you'll be able to make a black hole capable of sucking in half the planets in the solar system. Then you threaten to push the button if they don't give you the keys to the world and a lifetime supply of cherry-flavored Pez.

▷ RIP THE FABRIC OF SPACE-TIME

The universe we live in is made up of at least four dimensions: length, width, depth, and time. Altogether these four dimensions are called "space-time." Some scientists think that there are also other dimensions, such as chocolate pudding and bad monkey, but those aren't important right now.

What's important is that scientists also suspect that ours is not the only universe. There may be other universes that exist side by side with our own. All you have to do is cut a hole in the fabric of space-time, and you might be able to travel to other universes. Or you might open a gate that gives billions of giant alien spiders direct access to earth. Or the entire planet might get sucked through the hole like a watermelon through a drinking straw and then blasted into the middle of an exploding supernova named Ralph.

Real Spider

The point is that nobody knows for certain what would happen, and you can use this uncertainty to cause fear and panic among the people, who will then want to bring you fluffy pillows and bags of cash to stop you from annihilating the earth.

So how do you rip a hole in the fabric of space-time? I'm not entirely sure, but I've heard it can be done with a device known as a "continuum transfunctioner," which is a mysterious and powerful device whose mystery is exceeded only by its power. If you can lay your hands on one of these babies, you will be the only thing standing between the universe and completely violent destruction.

▷ DIG A TUNNEL TO THE EARTH'S MOLTEN CORE

Have you ever dug a hole in your backyard to see if you could make it to China? You didn't make it, did you? I'll bet you stopped before you even dug deep enough for a decent underground fortress. But I don't blame you or anything. Digging is hard work.

Besides, you never would have made it to China anyway. Before you got even halfway to China you would have been engulfed in molten lava, which is not a fun way to spend the last few seconds of your life. And

you might have created a massive volcano that would spew lava and boulders and hot gasses into the atmosphere and cause worldwide earthquakes, wiping out cities and possibly even destroying all of civilization.

And you thought you were just going to take some sandwiches to the nice kids in China. Little did you know that your tunnel was also a pretty awesome doomsday device. WHEW!

Unfortunately, as you already noticed, digging is hard work. And you don't want to end up burned to a cinder if you accidentally break through the earth's upper mantle to its superheated liquid metal core.

Better to get someone else to do it for you. This is why you have evil robots (see EVIL ROBOTS 101) and grunts (as described in the last chapter). That's right... your robots and grunts can be digging a really deep hole in the backyard for you while you relax in your jammies and slippers, watching cartoons and snarfing Cheez Doodles.

Don't forget, though...your grunts and robots need to stop digging *before* they reach the earth's core. That way you can *threaten* to have them dig the last few feet

and destroy the planet. If they *actually* reach the earth's core, you'll have a massive volcano in your backyard and can kiss your Cheez Doodles good-bye.

▷ MAKE GRAY GOO

Have you heard of nanotechnology? If not, nanotechnology means building stuff on a very, very small scale. Microscopic stuff. Like tiny robot clowns with tiny robot clown cars and tiny robot puppies. Yeah, I know. Scientists wouldn't really build microscopic robot clowns. But I would. Then I'd spend all day watching them in the microscope. I like tiny robot clowns.

But that's neither here nor there. You can use nanotechnology to create a doomsday device called "gray goo." To do this, you create a nano-robot that will use the matter around it to construct more nano-robots. Those nano-robots then create more nano-robots, which create more and more, and so on and so forth. They will eat everything in the environment—trees, buildings, people, telephone poles, sushi bars, unicycles, party hats, etc.—turning it all into a gray goo of nano-robots.

And be sure to give your nano-robot a really frightening name, like "Deathbot" or "Planet Melter 9000." If you call it "Stephanie," nobody will be frightened enough to let you take over the world.

▷ CREATE A MUTANT VIRUS THAT CAUSES ALL KITTENS TO GO INSANE

You don't need to rely on me to come up with all the great ideas. You can get creative and come up with some pretty nifty ideas yourself. Like this one: invent a virus that makes kittens think that human faces are made out of Fancy Feast, thereby creating flesh-eating zombie kittens. Then unleash it on the world's kittens, which will begin attacking the faces of unsuspecting humans, causing a worldwide zombie-kitten apocalypse. Or *threaten* to unleash it. Don't actually unleash it, please. I like my kitten and would not want her to attack my face. I would have to destroy her if she did.

▷ BREED BEES THAT ARE ADDICTED TO FAST FOOD

Or how about this one? Create a new strain of bees that eat only fast food, and threaten to release them into the wild, where they will breed with regular honey bees. If bees stop pollinating flowers and start pollinating cheeseburgers, the plants we rely on for food will stop producing anything and the human food chain will grind to a halt, thereby destroying all human life on earth.

▷ YOUR TURN

Now it's your turn to see how creative you can be. Take a few minutes to see if you can think of your own ways to make the earth uninhabitable by humans. Being the generous and lazy person I am, I left you a few more blank pages at the end of the book to write down your own fiendishly clever ideas for new ways to…"Help! There's a hamster in my undies!"

t happens every time. You're just about to hatch your plan to blow up the moon, and you find you've got some super spy running around your lab trying to disable your space missile with a package of chewing gum and a credit card.

In other words, as you start trying to take over the world, you are going to find yourself dealing more and more with pesky secret agents. And unless you want the good guys to win, you're going to need to need to know how to defeat them. Whether they are from the CIA, MI6, the FBI, the NSA, the YMCA, the PB&J, or the LOLCATS, you need to be prepared with a plan to bring them down.

Now, when it comes to dealing with secret agents, I have a mantra. A slogan. A motto. A thing I like to say. A lot. And it's this: "What you don't do is just as important as what you do do."

Don't get me wrong. What you do do is important, sure. What you do do in the morning, and what you do do every afternoon, and what you do do every night is important.

What? What's so funny? Are you laughing about "do do in the morning"? Would you please stop? I'm trying to explain something here. As I was saying, it's important what you do do, BUT…

WHAT? Now you're laughing at my "do do but"?

Will you please pay attention? What I was *trying* to say is that it is very important what you DON'T do when it comes to dealing with those sports-car-driving, tuxedo-wearing, license-to-kill types. And to make it as easy as possible for you, I spent several weeks watching spy-thriller movies and eating popcorn and Whoppers so that I could make this list.

THINGS TO NOT DO WHEN DEALING WITH SECRET AGENTS

DON'T DO: Tie them up, hang them from a slowly lowering chain over the "pit of doom," and then leave the room. Secret agents are great at escaping at the last minute and then coming back to thwart your plans.

DO DO: Tie them up and throw them in the pit of doom. Then you can laugh maniacally and go about your business of planning to crush and destroy things.

DON'T DO: Have ventilation ducts in your underground fortress that are large enough for a person to crawl through. The good guys like to sneak in through ventilation ducts.

DO DO: Install ventilation ducts that are only big enough for a hamster. And line them with razor wire in case your nemesis decides to infiltrate your fortress with a remote-controlled hamster.

DON'T DO: Install a self-destruct device in your stronghold with a big, red button labeled "SELF-DESTRUCT ACTIVATOR. DO NOT PUSH."

 DO DO: Install a trap door over the pit of doom with a big, red trap door opener button on the wall next to it labeled "SELF-DESTRUCT ACTIVATOR. DO NOT PUSH."

 DON'T DO: Put a large, red, digital countdown timer on your doomsday device so the good guys know how long they have to deactivate it.

 DO DO: Put a large, red, digital countdown timer on an air conditioner or a barrel of pickles to distract your nemesis from the real doomsday device until it's too late. If you absolutely *must* install a countdown timer on your real doomsday device, make it a small blue one or, better yet, cover it with something disgusting that no one would want to touch, like fake plastic doggie doo or a picture of your brother's room. When the good guys see *that*, they'll be too busy throwing up to disable the timer, leaving you plenty of time to flee in your escape pod before the island goes kablooie.

 DON'T DO: Challenge your enemy to hand-to-hand combat, a sword duel, or any other one-on-one fight. They might be more skillful than you. Definitely do not fight them on the edge of a cliff or a catwalk over the pit of doom. Only total n00bs do that.

 DO DO: Have your Legions of Terror (or is that your Happy Bunny Brigade?) overwhelm and destroy your enemy while you sit back and watch from a safe distance. Preferably on TV. With a cherry-banana Slurpee in one hand, a copy of *Super-Villain Quarterly* in the other, and a devilishly wicked smile plastered across your face.

 DON'T DO: Give public tours of your secret underground fortress, or allow repairmen and delivery men onto the premises.

DO DO: Keep the location of your underground fortress a secret. Deliveries should be made to your box at the post office, where your henchmen can pick them up. All maintenance and repairs should be done by your own staff of plumbers, electricians, and engineers. And they should all be dressed as chickens. Just because.

 DON'T DO: Throw a masquerade ball in your honor, so your nemesis can sneak in wearing a mask and mingle as one of your invited guests.

 DO DO: Invite your nemesis to a black-tie ball in their honor, and when they walk through the door, drop a safe on them. Or an anvil. Or a grand piano. Or a plumber dressed as a chicken.

 DON'T DO: Build a single doomsday device, ensuring some master spy can foil your plan by destroying your only weapon.

DO DO: Build at least two identical doomsday devices so you have a backup if the first one is destroyed. And keep them in different locations. And by "different locations" I don't mean "in the closet and under the bed." I mean, like Hawaii and Disney World. Hey, if you're going to hide your doomsday devices, you might as well hide them in places you want to go. After all, if you hide your backup doomsday device in someplace like Baghdad or Fresno, you might actually have to go there.

 DON'T DO: Have in your fortress a moat, swamp, pond, or river filled with deadly sharks, piranhas, crocodiles, barracudas, water snakes, etc. Your nemesis might turn the tables on you and push you in.

 DO DO: Have a moat or swamp or pond or river filled with speedboats and bathroom mirrors. Secret agents can never resist speedboats or bathroom mirrors. They'll be so distracted by driving the speedboats that they'll forget all about the doomsday devices. And they'll be so busy looking at themselves in the bathroom mirrors that they won't see where they're going, and they'll crash into a wall and explode in a huge fireball of gasoline and fiberglass and chicken suits.

A FINAL NOTE ON DON'T DO VS. DO DO

When hatching your master plan and trying to protect yourself from the secret agents who want to stop you, there are many things you might do but shouldn't, and lots of them are not on the list above. So you need to be able to figure out for yourself if any given option should be on the don't do list or the do do list.

One way to decide is to ask yourself if a plan is so dumb that your average cocker spaniel would know better. In other words, ask yourself, "What would a doggy do? Would a doggy do *this,* or would a doggy do *that?*" Once you have the answer to the question, "What would a doggy do?" you'll know whether it's a don't do or a do do. As long as your do do list is the same as the doggy do do list, secret agents will be unable to stop you and you will be one step closer in your quest for world domination and ultimate power.

> STEP 9 1/2 <

YOUR EVIL
TRADEMARK

ave you ever noticed that whenever you see a picture of somebody who's truly evil, there's always something especially memorable about them? Remember Darth Vader's black helmet and cape? How about Adolf Hitler's funky little mustache? Cruella de Vil's black-and-white hairdo? Dora the Explorer's little purple backpack? Yeah. You know what I'm talking about.

Well, there's a name for this, and it's called Fred. Okay, it's not really called Fred, but it would be funny if it were. No, it's actually called a *trademark*. When Superman put a big ol' *S* on his chest, he created a trademark. When Mickey Mouse got those giant ears with the red pants and the yellow shoes, that was his trademark. When Captain Hook got his hook and named himself Captain Hook. Right. Trademark.

Now, if you want to take over the world, you're going to want people to remember you. Which means you're going to need to make your own trade-mark. That doesn't mean you're going to need to put a big *E* for "Evil" on your chest or wear a little purple backpack. That would be silly. Besides, we already covered what you're going to wear earlier in the book.

No, what it means is that you're going to come up with *the thing that people remember you for*, such as your diabolical laugh, your evil eye, your slogan, your theme song, and so on. And I'm going to show you how to do it. Right here. Really soon.

Except I'm kind of hungry right now. So if you don't mind, I'm going to go get a sandwich, and then I'll come back and show you how to create your trademark. Would that be all right? It would? Gee, thanks!

Hey, would it be all right if I take a nap after lunch too? Wow, thanks. You're so kind and generous today.

Okay, so I'll be back in just a bit. In the meantime, I'm going to leave you with these pictures to color until I get back. See you soon!

Yawn! I'm back. Thanks. That was an awesome nap. I feel so much better now. So where was I? Oh, yeah. Your trademark.

Okay, so here's the deal. There are a bunch of different ways to create your own special evil trademark. You can even have more than one trademark if you want. Here are some ideas to choose from.

YOUR EVIL CATCHPHRASE

A catchphrase is something you like to say a lot, especially right before you are about to do something particularly wicked. These days, all the good villains have one. For example, the Riddler always likes to say, "Riddle me this…" The Borg on *Star Trek* like to say, "Resistance is futile." Dr. Claw always says, "I'll get you next time, Inspector Gadget!" Oh, and Barney always says, "I love you. You love me. We're a happy family." Man, that's evil.

So how do you come up with a good catchphrase, exactly? Well, here are a few rules of thumb:

1. Make it positive. In other words, you don't want a catchphrase like "Curses! Foiled again!" or "You beat me this time!" No, you need a more upbeat catchphrase that shows how powerful and amazing you are. You want something like "Prepare to lose," or "Bow down before my power."

2. A good catchphrase should be related to your power. For example, if you have a Giant Flame Ray Blaster Thingy, your catchphrase might be something like "Things are about to get hot." If, on the other hand, you have a Giant Ice Beam Blaster Thingy, you might say, "Everybody chill."

3. It's okay to be arrogant, but don't exaggerate. In other words, don't say, "I am invincible!" unless you are actually invincible. Don't say, "Nothing can stop me!" unless you are actually unstoppable. It could be embarrassing if you are stopped.

4. Keep it short. The best catchphrases are just three or four words. Anything longer than this and your catchphrase may bore the very people you are trying to impress. "You don't know the power of the dark side of the Force," is nice, but at twelve words long, how many times are you really going to want to say it? I recommend you try something punchier, like "Surrender the booty."

5. Statements are better than questions. Sure, you could have a catchphrase like "Who's ready for the hammer?" But your enemies might say, "Not me, thanks." And then where are you? Better to make it a statement, as in "It's Hammer Time!" Wait. I think that one's already been used.

Deciding on your evil catchphrase is only the first step. Next you need to use it so that everyone remembers it. Here are a few tips on how to deliver your catchphrase like a pro.

need catch phrase

1. Practice your catchphrase in the mirror before trying it out in public. Practice it over and over until you feel you've got it right.

2. Enthusiasm counts. Say it like you mean it. Put some feeling into it, especially if that feeling is joy at the humiliation of your enemies.

3. Use it as often as possible. What difference does it make if you drive everyone crazy? It's your catchphrase, and the more you use it, the more people will remember it. And you.

YOUR DIABOLICAL LAUGH

The best evil villains also have a great, wicked-sounding laugh. Imagine how a witch cackles after she casts an evil spell, or how a Mad Scientist might throw his head back and laugh at the sky after bringing his monster to life, or how a Super-Villain might laugh after the hero falls to his doom. That's the kind of laugh you want.

Now imagine how Mickey's pal Goofy laughs when he finds a nickel on the sidewalk, or how Elmo laughs when he gets tickled. That's *not* the kind of laugh you want.

Your laugh should never sound like "Huh-yunk!" or "Nyuk, nyuk, nyuk!" And it should definitely not be a "Snork!" or a "Whee-hee-hee." A better choice would be a deep and throaty "Mwahahahahah!" Or a loud, wall-shaking "Ahhhh ha ha ha ha ha ha!" Or a high-pitched, cackling laugh that sends chills down the backs of everyone who hears it. It can even be a deadly sounding "Heh heh heh heh heh!"

Your laugh can be short and sweet, or it can go on and on. The length is entirely up to you. But I'll say this…the longer your laugh is, the more likely it is to scare the bejeebies out of people.

Like your catchphrase, your diabolical laugh is something you need to practice in the bathroom mirror. You'll want to do it over and over until you get it exactly right.

You might even want to record your laugh on video so that you can play it back to make sure it sounds the way you think it does. Just be sure not to put that video on the Internet. No one ever takes a villain seriously if their diabolical laugh practice video is on the Internet where people can make fun of it.

YOUR EVIL EYE(BROW)

Some facial expressions are cute and sweet, while others can burn a hole right through you, especially the expressions of evil robots with laser eyeballs. But even if an expression doesn't literally burn a hole through you, it might still make you want to crawl into a hole and whimper. And every villain worth his salt—whatever that means—needs a good evil expression.

So ask yourself, what kind of evil expression can you make? Can you raise one eyebrow and stare creepily at your opponent like this?

Can you purse your lips
and squint like this?

Can you cross your eyes
and stick your tongue out like this?

Well, as you can see, that last one
was not particularly evil. So don't do it. But if
you can sneer, or if you can open your eyes wide and
flare your nostrils, one of these could be
your trademark expression. If not,
consider a pair of dark, evil-looking
sunglasses, like these.

YOUR EVIL INSIGNIA

I figured that when I wrote "YOUR EVIL INSIGNIA,"
you were probably going to ask something like,
"Where's the bathroom?" or maybe even, "Can I have
a piece of candy?" That's what kids are always asking.
"Can I have some candy? Can I have some candy? Can
I? Huh?" They never ask anything smart like "What's

the square root of 83?" or "Can you show me how to reload a laser cannon?" No. It's always "Where's the bathroom? Can I have some candy?"

The bathroom is over there. And, no, you can't have any candy. Not right now, anyway. Once you take over the world, you can have all the candy you want.

Now, what you should really be asking is "Huh? What's an insignia?" Good question. An insignia is a symbol of your personal power, such as a crown, or a flag, or a badger. You know how kings and queens wear crowns, and countries fly flags, and police officers wear badgers? What? What do you mean police officers don't wear badgers? Of course they do. Shiny, silver badgers, right there on their uniforms.

Ohhhh...I see what's going on here. The editor has been playing her own little joke on me, and every time I type the word *badger* without an *r*, she adds an *r* so that it reads *badger*. Well, that's fine. We don't need no stinkin' badgers, anyway.

Your insignia could be whatever kind of symbol you want it to be. It could be a patch on your shoulder or your hat. It could be painted on the sides of your personal fleet of sports cars and jets. Here are some examples of insignias you might have seen.

Now, those are all "normal" insignias. Normal insignias are for normal people. But you aren't exactly normal, or you wouldn't be reading this. So you don't want a normal insignia. You want an evil insignia. Like these:

So get cracking. You know what those blank pages at the back of the book are for. That's right; they're for evil doodles.

YOUR EVIL THEME SONG

Why is it that the good guys all have theme songs, but the bad guys never do? You know, like Spider-Man has "Spider-Man. Spider-Man. Does whatever a spider can." And Batman has "Duh nuh nuh nuh nuh nuh nuh nuh, nuh nuh nuh nuh nuh nuh nuh nuh, Batman!" But can you name me one villain who has a theme song? I didn't think so.

It's not fair, I tell you. And I'm out to change all that and make sure that from now on every villain gets his or her own theme song. An evil theme song.

So how do you make an evil theme song, exactly? Easy, take a regular song and change the words to make them evil. It's especially evil if you take a sweet, innocent little baby song and give it rotten, twisted lyrics. Like this. Do you know this song?

Row, Row, Row your boat,
gently down the stream,
merrily, merrily, merrily, merrily,
life is but a dream.

Well, what if you changed it like this:

Crush, crush, kill, destroy.
Everybody scream.
Soon I'll rule the planet
with my giant laser beam.

Or how about this one?

Yankee Doodle went to town
Riding on a pony,
stuck a feather in his hat
and called it macaroni.

You could change it like this:

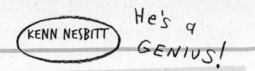
> Doctor Dreadful (or whatever your
> name is) crushed the town
> with his mutant minions,
> now he is the overlord
> of all the world's dominions.

See? Isn't this fun? And you can do it with any song you like. Heck, you can even make your own evil "theme poem" if you want. Like this:

> Roses are red.
> Prepare to be dead.

OTHER WAYS OF CREATING YOUR TRADEMARK

Insignias, theme songs, catchphrases, diabolical laughter, and evil looks aren't the only trademarks you can create. All the things you do—from the way you dress, to the way you comb your hair, to the way you dispatch your nemeses before breakfast—are things people will remember you for, which means any of them can be your special trademark. So whenever you make a decision on anything the public is going to see or hear about you, remember to first ask yourself, "Where's my little purple backpack?"

TRADEMARK IDEAS

1. PART HAIR ON SIDE
2. WALK WITH LIMP
3. HOLD A PET HAMSTER
4. HMMM...

A t last. You've conquered the world and you're ready to enjoy the fruits of your labor. Wait, that doesn't sound right. I mean, fruit is good and everything, better than vegetables anyway. Imagine if I said, "It's time to enjoy the vegetables of your labor." That would just be wrong. And, honestly, is fruit *that* much better? How about this instead? "It's time to enjoy the Gummi Bears of your labor." Yeah. That's better.

Anyway, here's the point. If you've followed my instructions up to this point, you should now be the ruler of the planet and have all the world's resources at your command. And that means it's now time to take advantage of your position of power and privilege.

You can spend vast and unreasonable sums of cash on anything you like, including mansions, sports cars, jets, islands, and those little chocolate cupcakes with the creamy white filling.

With so much money at your disposal and so many things to spend it on, you really need to make a list of what's most important. Otherwise you could end up spending a billion dollars on unnecessary trinkets and knickknacks that just clutter up the living room and make it hard to find the TV.

This handy guide will show you what's most important to spend your hard-won booty on and help you select only the very best of each.

200,000,003

37,555

1003

7.5

2

HOW MUCH IS A BILLION DOLLARS ANYWAY?

Before you start trying to spend a billion dollars, it helps to have some idea of exactly how much money that is so that you'll know how much money you'll want to spend each day. Since I enjoy thinking about vast quantities of money so much, I'll break it down for you.

1 Billion Dollars = 1000 x 1 Million Dollars

In other words, if you spend one million dollars every day, seven days a week, it will take you one thousand days—nearly three years—to spend a billion dollars. Obviously a million dollars a day is not nearly fast enough.

If you spend ten million dollars every day, seven days a week, it will still take you one hundred days—over three months—to blow through the entire billion. Probably still not fast enough.

If you spend thirty-five million dollars a day, you can get through an entire billion in less than a month. That's enough time that you can have lots of fun buying whatever you want, but not so long that you'll get bored with spending.

So now the question is: How can you spend thirty-five million dollars every day? Here's how.

BE UNREASONABLE

As world ruler, there will be plenty of time to spend billions or even trillions of dollars on stuff for your subjects;

stuff like bread and cabbages and pictures of you. So you should spend your first billion dollars just on yourself.

And before you start spending money on practical things like mountain hideaways and space stations, it's important that you spend an unreasonably huge amount of money on something completely ridiculous. What's the most ridiculous and unreasonable thing you can think of? How about a lifetime supply of gold-plated pickle-jar openers? Or a hundred thousand hand-carved sculptures of a chicken playing Ping-Pong? Perhaps enough Fruity Pebbles to fill the Grand Canyon?

wow! Great idea!

If your first purchase is ridiculous and unreasonable enough, it will send a message to the world's population that you can do whatever you want and they darned well better get used to it. More importantly, all future purchases will seem completely reasonable by comparison. When you order a fleet of a hundred new Ferrari sports cars for your personal use, everyone will think, "Thank goodness we don't have to carve any more of those chicken sculptures!"

Now that you've gotten that out of your system, let's

take a look at the more reasonable purchases you're going to want to make.

GETTING AROUND

World leaders need to travel, and to travel you're going to need transportation. Transportation can include anything that helps you get from place to place quickly, including jets, helicopters, sports cars, evil ponies, and so on.

But you don't just want to travel. You want to travel in style. So for each of these purchases, you need to think in terms of millions of dollars. For example, all the best sports cars cost about a million dollars each. If a sports car costs less than a million dollars, you don't want it. If, on the other hand, you find a nice sports car that costs a million dollars, you should order thirty-five of them right away, and then you'll be done spending money for the day and can go back to playing Go Fish with your robots and toasting marshmallows on their flamethrowers.

Now, there are two ways to spend a million dollars

or more on a sports car. One is to buy thirty-year-old limited edition collectible sports cars, and the other

is to buy brand-new sports cars. Locating expensive old sports cars takes more of the time that you'd rather spend playing Whac-A-Mole, so I suggest you go for the new ones instead. In particular, I recommend the McLaren F1 or the Bugatti Veyron, each of which will set you back a cool million and have top speeds of around 250 miles per hour. Wheeeeeee!

Private jets, as you may have guessed, cost a lot more than sports cars. A decent private

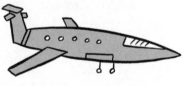

jet is going to cost you at least ten million dollars, but probably more. I recommend finding a sleek jet that costs, say, eighteen million dollars and ordering two of them. Be sure to ask for a million-dollar discount for buying two. That way they will cost exactly thirty-five million, and you'll be able to take the rest of the day off. If you buy four of them, you can take the next day off as well.

Helicopters, sadly, don't usually cost nearly as much as jets. These days you can buy a decent helicopter for a mere half-million dollars and an amazingly spiffy helicopter for only a million dollars. 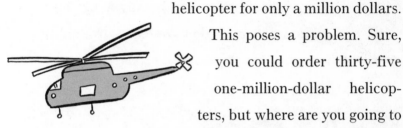 This poses a problem. Sure, you could order thirty-five one-million-dollar helicopters, but where are you going to put them all? And how are you ever going to use that many helicopters?

Luckily, there are still a few helicopters that cost seven or eight million dollars apiece, such as the Eurocopter AS332 Super Puma. It's a beautiful piece of flying machinery that is perfectly suited for flying your enemies out to sea and dropping them from very high altitudes. At these prices, you'll only need to buy four or five helicopters before you can go spend the rest of the day watching cartoons on the Internet.

As for the evil ponies, I'm not really sure if there is such a thing, but it sounds so perfect that even if there isn't, there should be. And they should cost thirty-five million dollars each, just to make things easy for new world rulers trying to spend a billion dollars in less than a month.

If you can't find an evil pony dealership in your hemisphere, I recommend hiring a genetic engineer to design evil ponies just for you. And be sure to pay him thirty-five million dollars so that you can move on to your next purchase.

YOUR NEW HOME(S)

When you're not traveling, you're going to want some-place nice to live. In fact, you're really going to need several nice places. Fortunately, very nice homes only cost about five million dollars apiece. That means you can buy seven beautiful houses in the nicest places in the world—places like Beverly Hills, California; and Paris, France; and Spokane, Washington—for only thirty-five million.

But buying seven homes is a lot of work. Maybe you don't want to spend all that time looking at pictures of five-million-dollar homes with their swimming pools and tennis courts and guesthouses and four-car garages.

Wouldn't it be so much simpler if you could buy just three twelve-million-dollar mansions? Of course it would.

Just so we're clear, a mansion is a ridiculously large house with twenty or thirty bedrooms, a ballroom, an indoor swimming pool, acres of lawns and sculpted hedges, lots of super-expensive paintings on the walls, indoor mini-golf, indoor go-karts, and a partridge in a pear tree.

Mansions typically cost more than regular nice houses, so you can plan to spend anywhere from ten to twenty-five million dollars on each one, making your shopping so much easier. If you buy mansions instead of just fancy houses, you will only need to buy two or three of them. Isn't that simpler? Of course it is.

Now, if you are so eager to get back to eating nachos on the couch in your jammies that you can't be bothered to even shop for two or three mansions, you might think that you could just shop for a castle instead. After all, castles are even bigger than mansions, so they must cost loads more money, making it that much easier for you to get through that entire billion before it burns a hole in your pocket.

Sadly, it just isn't so. The trouble is that there just

aren't that many castles in the world, and most of the ones that are for sale are old, musty, and crumbling. And they don't cost nearly enough. No, if you want to buy something that costs more than a mansion, the next logical step up is a private island.

Even the smallest private islands cost a million or more. And if you look in warmer climates like the South Pacific or the Bahamas, you can easily find islands that cost 35, 50, or even 150 million dollars or more. With prices like that, you could get several days' shopping done all at once.

You might even be able to kill two birds with one stone, so to speak. If you look carefully, you can find private islands with mansions on them, so you won't have to direct your minions to build you a house after you buy the island.

Houses, mansions, castles, and islands aren't the only places you can live. You can also buy entire mountains, though there are surprisingly few of these for sale. I also think it would be incredibly cool to buy your very own space station, though this one purchase might cost you more than your entire billion, so I'd think carefully before ordering one of these. After all, you want to have something left over to buy life's other necessities, such as pizza and chocolate. Which brings us to what I recommend you spend another hundred million or so on...

FOOD AND CLOTHING

Yes, yes, yes. I know what you're thinking. You're thinking, "Isn't this book done yet?" No! And it won't be until I'm ready for another nap. Or maybe you're thinking, "Come on! You can't spend a hundred million dollars on food and clothes!" Think again. Here are just a few examples:

→ World's Most Expensive Suit: $25,000

→ World's Most Expensive Shoes: $3 million

→ World's Most Expensive Watch: $25 million

→ Being the World's Richest Evil Ruler: Priceless

See what I mean? As long as you stick with the most expensive of everything, you can easily spend millions of dollars on a stylish new wardrobe.

Food, on the other hand, can't possibly cost millions of dollars, can it? Of course it can! If you want food that costs actual millions of dollars, all you have to do is hire several of the highest-paid chefs in the world and fly them to wherever you are to personally prepare your food. These guys charge a *lot* of money. And, of course, you insist that they only use the most expensive ingredients in the world. This way, with very little effort, you should be able to spend over a million dollars a day on food, or thirty-five million dollars in one month. Yum.

TOYS, GADGETS, AND OTHER JUNK AND STUFF

Of course, there's more to life than just housing, transportation, food, and clothes. You also need lots of toys and gadgets and other junk and stuff like that. But somehow I don't think you are going to need my help figuring out how to spend millions of dollars on toys and gadgets. I'll bet you've got that one covered. Am I right? Of course I am.

STEP 10

HOW TO RULE
THE WORLD

ongratulations! At last, you have taken over the world. And it only took ten easy steps. Okay, so there might have been a couple more steps in there somewhere, but that doesn't really matter, because now that you've conquered the planet, you can relax and enjoy life with your friends. Except for one little thing...

YOU DON'T HAVE ANY FRIENDS

Oh, shoot! Did I forget to tell you at the beginning of the book that once you take over the world, you won't have friends anymore? Sorry. My bad.

Oh, well, that's the way it goes when you rule the

planet. Some of your old friends are jealous of your success, and the rest don't like you anymore because you're so selfish, rotten, and despicable. You probably didn't even remember to give your friends their own countries for Christmas, did you?

If any of your old friends are still hanging around, it's not because they actually like you or anything; they just like the free ice cream and the occasional evil pony ride.

Which kind of makes you wonder, if you aren't going to have friends anymore, is it even worth going to the trouble of taking over the world? Sure, you've got lots of money, but don't they say that money can't buy love, happiness, and friendship? Without friends, what's the point of it all anyway?

Well, it's too late to start worrying about that now. You're in charge and everybody hates you, so you're just going to have to get used to it. Fortunately, this last chapter will show you how you can still have fun ruling the world, even when nobody likes you. And, after all, isn't that why you took over the world in the first place? To have fun? Of course it is. So here's how.

reminder: call Chuck

RULING THE WORLD THE FUN WAY

I've always thought that there are two kinds of people in the world: those who divide people into two kinds and those who don't. As you can tell, I'm the sort of person who divides people into two kinds. So when it comes to world rulers, I think there are two kinds: the fun kind and the kind who need to learn how to loosen up.

If you're already the fun kind of ruler, hopefully this chapter will show you how to have even more fun. If you're the kind who needs to loosen up a little, it will show you how to do that too.

First off, forget all that "ruling with an iron fist" business. I mean, who wants to have to walk around all day with an iron fist? That doesn't sound like fun at all. I'd much rather have a Rubber Mallet Fist, or a Play-Doh Fist, or a Chocolate Bunny Fist. If you try to rule with an iron fist, even your minions aren't going to like you, and they'll stop bringing you shiny toys and wheelbarrows of cash.

So instead of trying to rule the rotten, evil, despicable way, here are a few things you can do to rule the world the fun way.

▷ DECLARE LOTS OF NEW HOLIDAYS

Sure, you *could* immediately declare a new holiday in honor of yourself, but would it *really* be fun to celebrate Dr. Despicable Day? Okay, it might be fun for you, but everybody else would hate it, and then they'd want to topple your government and throw you into a giant vat of starving, crazed weasels.

Instead, I recommend declaring the most fun holidays you can think of. For example, you might declare National Cartoon Day, when everyone has to stay home and watch cartoons all day.

Or consider the following:

→ Underwear Hat Day: Announce that it's mandatory to wear your underwear on your head.

→ Sleepy Day: Make it illegal to wake up before noon.

→ National Singing Day: People have to sing everything they say.

→ Skipping Day: Proclaim skipping the only means of transportation. (No walking allowed!)

→ OR National Ice Cream Day.

→ OR Video Game Day.

→ OR Dress Like a Chicken Day.

→ OR See If You Can Get Your Whole Hand into Your Mouth Day.

me in chicken suit

See? With a little effort, I'll bet you could come up with dozens of new holidays.

I also recommend creating lots of new festivals, parades, celebrations, and desserts to go with your new holidays. That way everyone will be so busy celebrating and having fun all the time that they will completely forget to hate you.

Oh, and holidays don't have to be only once a year. You could make every Wednesday Ice Cream Social Day and make Monday Pancake Breakfast Day. The third Tuesday of every month could be Take the Day Off and Go to the Movies Day. See? Isn't it fun being in charge?

▷ RENAME EVERYTHING YOU WANT

In fact, when you're in charge, you get to decide what things are called. And I'm not talking about renaming streets and buildings and bridges in your honor. Nope. I'm talking about renaming chocolate to "spinach and Brussels sprouts." I've heard that spinach and Brussels sprouts are healthy for you. Start calling chocolate "spinach and Brussels sprouts," and you can enjoy a healthy plate of "spinach and Brussels sprouts" every day without ever getting tired of it.

Or why not rename stuff that's completely ridiculous to rename? Like Thursday. What might you call it? Oh, I don't know. How about Fleenday? Or Glonkday? Why? Because you can, that's why.

While you're at it, February's kind of hard to pronounce and spell, so why don't you change it to Bob. After all, April, May, and June are named after girls, but how many months are named after boys? Wouldn't it be more fair if the months were January, Bob, Dave, April, May, June, Kevin, and so on?

Of course, you don't have to limit yourself to month names and days of the week. You can rename states and countries you don't like. Have trouble spelling Zimbabwe? Shorten it to *Z*. Mississippi causing

problems for you? Rename it Stinkypinkyland just for the fun of it. Think New York is a dumb name? Change it to New Cheeseburger, or anything else you like.

Heck, you could even rename the earth, the sun, the moon, and the planets if you want to. Be creative. Look around and see what you can find that is in need of a new name, and give it one. After all, you are the supreme and absolute ruler of all the world, and people have to do what you say. And if you come up with really fun names for stuff, they're going to *want* to do what you say, because it's just so much fun.

▷ CHANGE THE LAWS

When you have absolute power, your word is law. That means you get to make up the laws, and everybody has to obey them.

Now, of course, you *could* pass a law requiring everyone to wear T-shirts with your picture on them and praise you all day long. But that's only fun until they storm your mansion and lock you up in your own dungeon.

Instead, you can now change the laws to make life more interesting. Of course, with all the weird laws out there right now, you'd have to think of some pretty unusual ones if you wanted them to be more fun than the ones already on the books.

For example, did you know that there are laws in the state of Georgia making it illegal to keep donkeys in bathtubs or carry ice cream cones in your back pocket on Sundays? Did you know that Rhode Island has a law making it illegal to throw pickle juice on a trolley? And in Denver, Colorado, it's unlawful to lend your vacuum cleaner to your next-door neighbor.

I know. You think I'm making those laws up, but I'm not. I read them on the Internet, so they must be true.

So if you're going to make laws that are more interesting than those, you're going to need to get pretty creative. Like this:

You could make it illegal to sell asparagus when the moon is full, and violators would have to dress like giant Oreo cookies for a week.

You could create a law requiring all cows to wear tutus and Viking helmets.

You could even make it illegal to catch fish with any body part other than your mouth. Oh, wait. They already have a law like that in Pennsylvania. Oh, well. Just do your best.

▷ CHANGE WHATEVER YOU WANT BECAUSE YOU FEEL LIKE IT

Whenever new rulers or leaders take over, they usually change stuff, but it's always boring stuff. They change the tax code, or health care laws, or dumb stuff like that. You have the opportunity to shake things up by being the first world leader to do things differently.

Sure, you could do something dull like require cars to use less fuel, but wouldn't it be more fun to tear down the White House and rebuild it to look like a giant rubber ducky? In fact, why not require all government buildings to look like enormous bath toys?

What if you replaced all public transportation with roller coasters and water slides?

What if all money had pictures of funny authors on it (hint, hint) instead of dead presidents?

What if schools were required to teach fun stuff like skateboarding and video game skills?

What if you could change anything you wanted, any way you wanted? Well, guess what? You can.

YOU'RE IN CHARGE NOW

That's right. You're in charge now. So make whatever changes you want.

Just make sure that whatever you decide to change, you have fun with it. Be sure to only change ordinary boring things into fun, exciting, and maybe even silly things. If you do that, why, then people will start to like you again. And when people start to like you, you'll have friends again. And everyone will want you to *continue* to rule the world.

And maybe, just maybe, they'll forget all about how evil and rotten and despicable you used to be and how you threatened to destroy the world. If you're lucky.

ABOUT THE AUTHOR

KENN NESBITT was born into the noblest of families, and made himself what he is today: a broken shell of a man, mumbling something about "enemies" and plotting his return to power. He was last seen hiding in a subbasement with a ten-year supply of frozen bologna sandwiches and his no-good, backstabbing cyborg manservant, Clyde. Writing this book was the happiest four days of his life.

And the drawings were cool, too.

ABOUT THE ILLUSTRATOR

ETHAN LONG was not born evil. He learned how to be villainous and treacherous from his older brother, who turned professional at age four. He has spent the last forty years of his life practicing good deeds and angelic ways, none of which you will find in this book. He lives in Orlando, Florida, and has no intention of ruling the world.

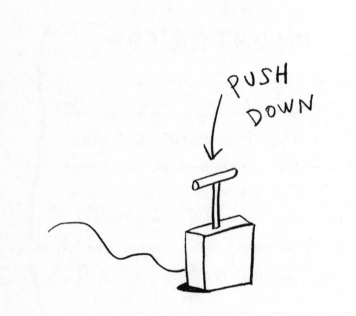

NOTES:

Dr. Fire the horrible

DESTRUCTION NOTES:

NOTES:

NOTES:

DESTRUCTION NOTES:

NOTES:

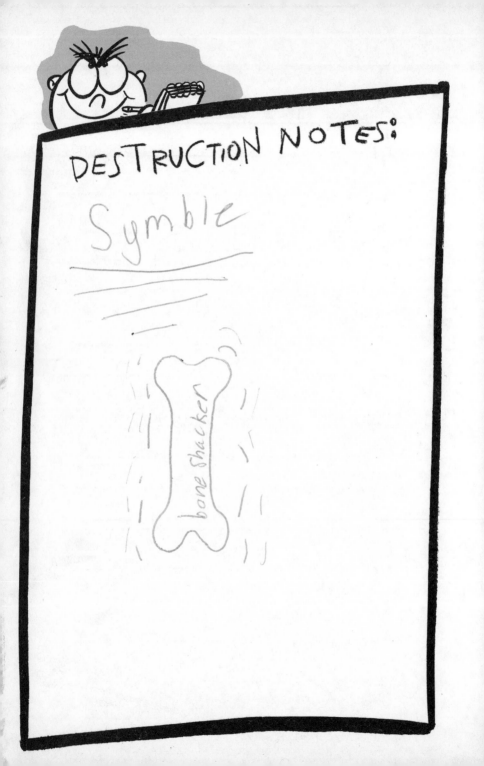

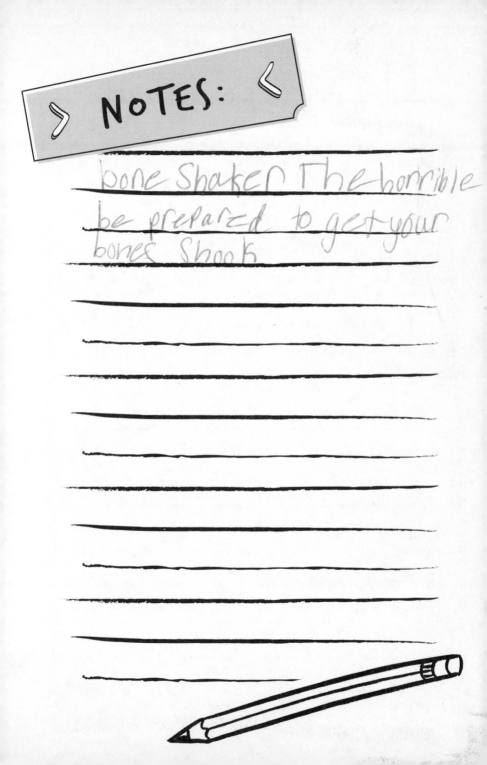

NOTES:

bone shaker The horrible
be prepared to get your
bones shook

DESTRUCTION NOTES:

NOTES:

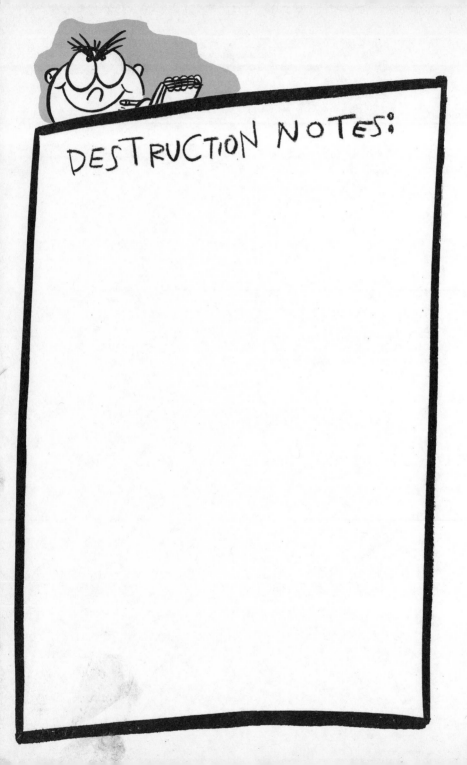

DESTRUCTION NOTES: